KAMYONISTAN

KAMYONISTAN

ROBERT HACKFORD

ATHENA PRESS
LONDON

ISBN 978 1 84748 372 0

First published 2008 by
ATHENA PRESS
Queen's House, 2 Holly Road
Twickenham TW1 4EG
United Kingdom

Printed for Athena Press

PART ONE

The Gates of Kamyonistan

At sunset, a huddle of lorries stood golden-windowed in the dusty truck stop, which lay just off the old main road approaching Damascus from Homs. Trailer lockers were open while meals were thrown together by weary long-haulers in that easy squalor of the wilderness. Tilt canopies sucked and billowed in an idle breeze, which tugged at the hissing blue flames of drivers' little gas stoves and carried fragments of their conversation away into the evening. Distant camels glided and flickered among the lorries, as cooking aromas and whiffs of hot diesel hung briefly in the air.

Only an hour before, in the evening sunlight, one of the lorries, a British ERF with a yellow tilt trailer, had made its way down the bare, brown folds of mountain. Ro, who was fifteen, had sat in the passenger seat and watched as his uncle, Norman, had held back the huge urge of his forty-tonner on the steeper descents. Double-declutching his way down the Twin Splitter gearbox, Norman had piloted his maroon EC11 off the mountain road and into the lane which led into the truck stop, which was in a transport zone known to Turkish drivers as 'Kamyonistan', with its enormous Islamic archway for an entrance.

'Better get these washed up before the light goes,' Norman said, gesturing at the pots and bowls. 'We'll eat in the restaurant tomorrow, when we've tipped.'

'I want to go and look at those camels,' Ro said.

'I don't know what they're doing here,' Norman replied. 'You don't see camels in this part of Syria any more. Let's do the dishes and see the camels after we've unloaded in the morning.'

The muezzin's call to prayer lifted on the evening air and echoed among the dusty palms. To Ro it sounded eerie and beautiful, and he paused to let the sound finish before starting his dishes.

By breakfast time it was already hot. Ro had been woken several times in the night by the noise of lorries rumbling and creaking across the unmade surface of the compound. Among the newcomers was a Dutchman called Kees, who was an old pal of Norman's. When Norman had been to the freight agents' building and sorted his papers out, he returned to find that Kees and Ro had stowed the kitchen away and were ready for work. Kees rode with them in the high 'Olympic' cab while Norman drove to a neighbouring compound which had a crane in it.

Under the blazing sun they set about stripping the trailer, which was a classic tilt with Long-Haul Services printed on each side. At 4 metres high, 2.5 metres wide and 13.6 metres long, it had drop sides and a heavy, soft plastic canopy covering a metal frame, like a tent. Removable wooden sideboards strengthened the sides. At each corner a strong plastic tape ran down through a series of eyelets to join the TIR cord at the bottom. From the hinged aluminium drop sides protruded staples over which metal eyelets in the hem of the canopy fitted, secured by the plastic-coated wire TIR cord, which threaded right round the trailer and fastened at the rear with a seal. At the front and back were blue and white TIR plates. A double wheel carrier was slung under the rear of the chassis, and capacious side lockers served as a kitchen and a toolbox.

Once they had undone the sides, it was necessary to climb up on to the top, pull up the heavy sheet and fold both sides onto the roof. When that was done they had to roll the sheet to the front of the trailer. A tilt has no solid roof, only rails and poles, so finding somewhere to stand on, or to push from, was not easy. Ro sat astride the cantrail and pushed with all his might, but couldn't budge the heavy mass of folded plastic. Sweating profusely, Kees and Norman eased it foot by foot. Next, using a lump hammer, they knocked out the cantrails, took out the roof poles, the wooden sideboards and the pillars; then they opened the drop sides, which were hinged to the rave. Lastly, they released all the webbing straps that had restrained the load of machinery on its journey from England. Now the crane could safely lift off the machines.

'Throw all the stuff in the trailer,' Norman announced, when the load was off. 'We can rebuild it this evening when it's cooler. I don't know about you, Kees, but I can feel a beer coming on.'

The late October sun was high by the time they returned to their spot in the compound where they parked under a palm tree. They washed in one of the wash blocks and headed for the restaurant, which overlooked the TIR parking. It had a veranda with tables and chairs. Some of the chairs were draped with *shisha* pipes. The proprietor appeared, drying a glass and introduced himself as Mehmet. He welcomed them warmly. '*Shay*?' he asked.

'Beer!' Kees said.

'*Shay*,' said Ro, whose journey across Turkey had accustomed him to the sweet tea known in Turkey as *chai*.

'Where are you going, Saudi?' Norman asked when they had sat down.

'No, here! I'm tipping here, in Kamyonistan, but they won't take it off till Tuesday.'

'Par for the course,' Norman said. 'You've normally got a fridge, why the tilt?'

'Had to swap trailers with someone. I'll get it back next trip. Where are you loading home from – Italy? You won't get a good load down here.'

'Funnily enough, I have!' Norman replied. 'I've got a reload from here. Payment's pretty safe this time, but I'll have to wait for the load. It's garments; not hanging ones, but jeans in cartons. I don't think they've made them yet!'

'And the boy, here?'

'Well,' Norman said hesitantly, glancing at Ro, 'his mum died last year and I'm looking after him. I had to bring him down with me because he got in with a bad crowd and drank too much. I have to keep an eye on him.'

'He'll need to keep an eye on you, then, I think.' Kees laughed. 'The amount you put away!'

'Why don't you investigate those camels, Ro?' Norman said. 'Find out what they're doing here.'

Ro wandered out into the parking compound. The sun was bright and the air was filled with dust and the smell of diesel. Dodging among the wagons, Ro went in search of the camels.

They were not to be found in the lorry park, so he went out into the road that led to the other compounds. The road was lined with palm trees. It had high kerbs and raised drain covers and a fearsome-looking speed ramp. A couple of lorries dozed at the side, their cab curtains drawn. Ro walked back to the restaurant, where Norman enquired about the camels.

'Try the livestock compound,' Mehmet suggested. 'The camels may be in transit. We only have tourist ones in Syria now.'

Ro followed Mehmet's directions, until he came to the livestock compound. This compound, Mehmet had informed him, was there for the large number of sheep that were exported from Turkey to Saudi Arabia, especially during Eid el-Adha, when sheep were slaughtered as part of the festival.

Just inside the compound gate he found the camels, their forelegs hobbled, next to a small truck. Ro approached shyly. A boy, about his own age, ran to greet him.

'*Misaa ilkheer! Ahlan wa sahlan!*' the boy said with a radiant smile. He wore a white, ankle-length jalabiya and a red and white *shamagh*, which was wound round his head.

'Hello,' Ro replied, holding out his hand. The boy shook it warmly and held on to it.

'Where are you from?' He asked this in English.

'England.'

'Ha!' said the boy, triumphantly. 'I can speak some English. I am from Egypt. We used to do camel treks on Sinai for tourists and I learnt lots of English.'

'Camel treks?'

'Yes. But now my grandfather is selling these in Aleppo. He's having trouble with the export papers.'

'Are they dangerous?' Ro asked.

'Come on,' the boy said, laughing. 'I'll show you.' Then Ro noticed that he only had one arm, the right one.

'What's your name?' the boy asked.

'Ro.'

'Ro. My name's Nuri.'

'Hello Nuri.'

'How old are you?'

'*Khamsatashar* – fifteen.'

'Same as me, then.'

Nuri hissed through the side of his teeth and gently pulled down the head rope of one of the camels. It hooted and knelt down. Next he dragged a wooden saddle with prominent pommels across the ground. 'You'll have to help me lift it. I've only got one arm.'

Ro helped him to lift it onto the camel's back. Under instruction from Nuri, Ro helped to secure the saddle with straps.

'Climb on,' Nuri urged. Ro was unsure.

'Is it safe?'

'Of course it is, if you hold on tight.' Ro sat in the saddle.

'What happened to your arm?' Ro asked, unable to contain himself any longer.

Nuri's face lit up, as if remembering a joyous meeting. 'I was struck by lightning!' he said, slinging his *shamagh* across one shoulder.

'Lightning?'

'Yes, all down one side. The hospital had to chop the arm off. Do you want to see?' Without waiting for an answer, Nuri lifted his jalabiya to his neck and pulled up his vest to reveal that his torso was scorched down the left side, the scorch marks running into the smooth, brown skin of his chest and tummy.

'How old were you?'

'Ten. Hold on!' The camel jacked itself up and nearly catapulted Ro from the saddle. Nuri led the placid beast round the compound with Ro happily surveying the world from aloft.

'How long are you staying, Ro?'

'A few days.'

'Good. You can come back.' When Ro was safely back on earth, Nuri showed him the camel feed. 'We feed them on hay mostly, but in the mountains we give them twigs and things.'

'Where's your grandfather now?'

'He's drinking with the sheep vet. I've got to unload this feed before he comes back.'

'I'll help you, come on.' The boys heaved down a few bales.

'I wish I'd brought my hat, the sun's blistering,' Ro grumbled. Nuri giggled and detached his *shamagh* from his shoulder; then, facing his new friend, he wound it round Ro's head and adjusted it carefully. Nuri's breath was sweet upon his face and their eyes met, dancing. 'It's perfect!' he said, laughing delightedly.

Ro kept it on and they unloaded more feed from the little truck. When Ro announced that he had to return to rebuild the tilt, he handed the head-cloth back to Nuri. Solemnly, Nuri wound it back round the boy's head, Beduin-style, and Ro marvelled at how deftly this was executed with just one arm.

'Now you try,' Nuri said, taking it off again and handing it to Ro. After several goes, Ro got the hang of it. Then Nuri shook his hand. 'Keep it, *saddiqi*, it's yours. You are my friend.'

'Thanks! I mean, *shukran*,' Ro said. The light, cotton material felt soft round his head. Ro sighed happily and they said their farewells.

'See you tomorrow,' Ro said.

'*Bokra, insha'allah* – tomorrow,' Nuri replied with a wave. A fanfare of Syrian multi-toned air-horns echoed across Kamyonistan announcing new arrivals, as Ro strolled back practising the donning of his *shamagh* with only one hand, as he had been taught.

Lorrying for Boys

Next morning, Norman, wearing jeans and an old T-shirt, 'ran the lorry up' for an hour at fast tick-over. Ro started the engine for him.

'800 revs should do it, Ro. If we're going to be here for a few days the last thing we want is flat batteries. Mind you, tomorrow I want to take the trailer round to the workshops and get a new side locker fitted.'

'What's wrong with the old one?'

'Rotten. The Syrians make a good job of this kind of thing. I had the camel-bar done at Homs, you know. Cheap, too.'

'Are you going to teach me how to drive?' asked Ro.

'Ah, yes!' Norman replied. 'That'll save running her up the next day, too. We'll have to find somewhere quiet.'

'There's an empty compound by the livestock one,' Ro said. He was a skinny kid with very fine, fair hair and violet eyes. His complexion was clear, if slightly sallow. Although of medium height, he was long in the leg, which meant that he could reach the pedals comfortably.

They found Kees and headed off to the drivers' souk. This turned out to be an Aladdin's cave of sundry trinkets, from horns that barked to magnificent copper dishes picturing the customer's own truck, copied from a treasured photograph, with the minarets of the Umayyad Mosque in Damascus showing in the background. Shelves were stacked with 'LONG VEHICLE' plates, some in Turkish reading *UZUN ARAC*. There were stainless steel exhausts, TIR plates, trailer winding handles, spare bundles of flex called susies, windscreen scarves, out of date atlases and rubber gloves. Elsewhere, they found leather jackets and folding stools, one of which they bought for Ro. Kees bought a set of long-handled brushes for cleaning trucks.

'I remember seeing copper dishes with trucks and mosques on them at Londra Camp,' Kees commented.

'Where's that?' Ro asked.

'Istanbul,' Norman put in. 'We gave it a wide berth on the way down. It used to be a king among truck stops, but not any more. It's just a little yard now; they've half-built hotels on the rest of it and then abandoned them.'

'Used to be good,' Kees added. 'Now, when we get back, are you going to test-drive these brushes for me?'

'All right,' Ro said. 'I'll do both wagons, but can I bring a friend to help?' The drivers laughed. 'OK then!'

They met a variety of vendors in the compound; a peanut seller rumoured to peddle wacky baccy, a flat bread seller, a leather belt seller and a man with a motorbike selling gas bottles.

'Hello! That looks like Jumbo's wagon,' Norman said as they approached their lorries. 'He must have just arrived. I hope he's got the kettle on. Looks as if you've got three wagons to wash, Ro. Better get your mate!'

Nuri was delighted to see Ro and greeted him with a hug. They found a couple of empty plastic five-litre containers and filled them with water from the shower block before returning to the lorries. Nuri applied himself to the lower cab panels and the chassis, while Ro climbed up and did the glass work. The long handles enabled them to reach the high sleeper cabs, but they left the trailers. It was hard work.

'You could earn a bob or two cleaning trucks,' Jumbo said. He was enormous, and had a straggly grey beard.

'Shall we?' Ro said. Nuri's radiant smile said 'Yes!' – and a truck-wash was born.

The Mediterranean sun was high and the drivers busied themselves with the routine tasks of the road; levels to check, bulbs to replace, prop-shafts to grease, cabs to sweep out. Then they cracked open cans of beer and sat in garden chairs.

'Jumbo's on the beach!' Norman laughed. It was, indeed, like a harbour beach. Before them lay a haven for a land-bound merchant navy of wagons swaying, lurching and wallowing in the wake of one another's dust from port to port. The midday call to prayer wailed above the rumble of diesel engines. Ro stowed the brushes and rejoined the drivers just as Jumbo was saying, 'She came out of the shower with nipples like Scammell wheel nuts.'

Ro missed the rest in a cacophony of Syrian air-horns. Jumbo finished. There was laughter. Ro and Nuri slipped away to play.

That evening, the drivers ate together in the restaurant. Mehmet, the proprietor, shook hands with them and they ordered kebab and chips from the Turkish waiter, Ramazan. Norman enquired, 'Any Turk beer, mate? Any Efes Pils?' Arabic pop music was playing at full blast and drivers were barking at each other jovially across the tables.

'Only just started driving, I had,' Jumbo was hooting. 'Early seventies, like; on my way to Pakistan. You could do Pakistan, then. Hits a bloody camel, don't I.'

'You're joking!'

'No. Well, the police capture me and stick me in a hole in the ground.'

'Blimey! What did you do?'

'Cacked myself, mate, with fear!'

'How did you get out?'

'Ba'sheesh, as usual.'

'Doesn't half make a mess of the wagon,' Norman said.

'What?'

'Camel.'

'There are plenty of them on the Saudi TAP-line road,' Kees put in. 'I've nearly hit them.'

'Saw half a bear in the road once, near Burgos in Spain,' Norman said.

'Blimey! Where was the other half?'

'Spread up the front of a Dutch wagon. Fridge, it was. Police was there and all that. Dunno what happened to the cloggy.'

'I hit a pink unicorn once and never felt a thing,' Jumbo said.

'What are you on about?'

'It was after a drink or two on the Bilbao boat, then a ten-hour shift down the road. But south of Madrid the pink unicorns started showing up.'

'He's right,' Kees said. 'Those Morocco runs didn't do any of us any good!'

Ro finished his *shwerma* and slipped into the night. Scattered groups of trucks were lit by little gas stoves and locker lights, where drivers were sharing meals under the stars. A crescent moon stood bright against the silhouette of one of the minarets that formed part of the compound wall. Tomorrow, he and Nuri would wash trucks.

Kamyonserai

The sun was already fiercely hot, even though it was October, when Norman fired up the big Cummins motor after breakfast. He'd always liked a Cummins on Middle East work because all the countries on the way down knew how to repair them. Norman told Ro that properly speaking, an ERF wasn't suited to the work because the plastic cab was too hot in summer and too cold in winter; but he'd paid next to nothing for this one and it was reliable. Ideally, he would have liked a left-hooker. Once the air pressure was up, he eased it forward between Jumbo's camping table and Kees's washing, then headed off to the workshops to have the trailer measured for its new side locker.

Ro and Nuri tended to the camels and left them with the grandfather, carrying their water containers and Kees's brushes. They decided to start in the compound next door, where the diesel pumps were situated near a brand new truck-washing machine. They filled their containers and staggered to the nearest lorry, which was a bonneted Lebanese Scania 140. The 36-year-old tractor unit was shabby, with a roof-mounted air-con and Trilex wheels. Its driver, Khalid, had loaded his standard Arab-style open trailer with cases of bottled water in Beirut docks a couple of days previously and had wound through the Lebanese capital in the midday heat before crawling up the mountain road behind the city on the road to Damascus. Khalid motioned the boys to sit with him at his trailer box and share the *shisha* pipe. Politely, Nuri declined and asked about washing the wagon.

'Later,' said the driver. 'Later there will be three trucks for you.' Like most drivers from Middle East countries, he had an assistant who helped with loading, repairs and cooking. Khalid's assistant returned from his prayers and stuffed his rolled prayer mat behind the passenger seat. Ro wanted to know where Khalid would go next.

'Dubai, *insha'allah*. Maybe wait here one week. Or two,' he added, resigned to the pace of his existence.

'What cargo will you take to Dubai?' Ro asked.

'Same,' laughed the Lebanese driver. 'Same water, different papers.' The driver's assistant gave a cry as two clouds of dust wove round the potholes towards them. It was the other Lebanese trucks. Saying their goodbyes, the lads ambled past the silent truck-wash.

A tall, dark youth wearing red shorts was sitting on a rail and watching them. As they drew close, he began half-heartedly to lob pebbles at them. Nuri put down his water and strode purposefully towards him and held out his hand, greeting him in Arabic. Scowling, the boy gave his name as Mahmout, the truck-wash proprietor's son. The mechanised truck-wash was out of commission, he said, broken. Mahmout stared unnervingly at Ro for a while. Then he slid off his rail and plonked himself in the seat of a derelict forklift truck. His bare, brown legs stuck out on either side of the steering wheel, which he drummed incessantly with his fingers. Ro and Nuri left him, lugging their heavy containers slowly across the compound.

The newly arrived Lebanese drivers called them over and they were engaged to work. The drivers taught them how to throw water up the sides of the cab using only their hands and minimal water. They even donated a nearly empty bottle of washing-up liquid. By the time they had finished they were hot and bothered.

They decided to empty their remaining water out and refill their containers nearer to base, to obviate the water transportation problem. Their next truck was a new Syrian Volvo, complete with a traditional, elaborately wrought camel-bar. While they were working, a man arrived and began to take photographs. 'Do you mind moving back a minute while I snap?' he called, waving his arm for them to move.

'OK. Just a moment,' Ro said obligingly.

'Oh! You're English!'

'Yes,' Ro said. 'Our trailer's being measured up for a locker. Who are you, a driver?'

'I used to be,' said the man. 'I'm Eric, by the way; I'm investigating Kamyonistan. Fascinating.'

'Why?'

'It's meant to be in the style of a medieval caravanserai, because cameleers and travelling merchants were basically medieval truckers, weren't they? I've been doing some homework on this truck stop because it's the only one I can think of that tries to unite the idea of a caravanserai with a truck stop.'

'Is that what you do?'

'Well, I'm a journalist for the trade press – you know, truck magazines. But recently I've done features on many of the big watering holes like Geiselwind in Germany and Londra Camp in Istanbul; also some old favourites in Spain, France and Italy.'

'England?'

'Don't even think about mentioning England and truck stops in the same breath! It's too embarrassing. England hates trucks.'

'That's what Uncle Norman says.'

'Britain could take a leaf out of the Seljuks' book…'

'Seljuks?'

'They ruled much of Turkey in the eleventh to thirteenth centuries and built caravanserais with taxpayers' money, to maintain the safe flow of trade.'

'For camel trains?'

'Yes, and mule-trains. Did you come across Turkey via Ankara and then go south to Aksaray?'

'Yes, that's where we topped up with diesel.'

'Well, if you turn right at Aksaray on the long and dusty road to Konya, you'll come across a magnificent caravanserai built in 1229 at the village of Sultanhani. It is huge and has been beautifully restored. Well worth a visit on the way home. What's your name, by the way?'

'I'm Ro, and this is my friend Nuri. He's a cameleer.'

'Is he?'

'Yes. His camels are in the livestock compound.'

'You don't want to be lugging this water about if you've got camels! Let them carry it – that's what they're for!'

Nuri's serene face glowed at the prospect of using his lifelong camel craft. The two boys looked excitedly at one another and fidgeted.

'You know,' Eric continued, 'even now, the Turks have an

important network of truck stops; not only in Turkey, but wherever Turkish drivers go. So there are "Turk parks", as British drivers call them, throughout Saudi Arabia in the south, Romania and Hungary in the north; and even in Azerbaijan, where there's a classic one at Ganja. There's a map on the wall in the café; I'll show you later if you like.'

'So camels are like the ghosts of trucks, then.'

'Ha! Sort of!' Eric then went on to explain that when Kamyonistan transport zone was planned, Saudi Arabia promised a large-ish mosque for the use of drivers. 'Most surprising of all,' Eric enthused, 'a wealthy consortium of architects with a zealous interest in Islamic architecture offered to design and subsidise an ambitious, experimental attempt to enclose the TIR parking compound in a giant caravanserai, complete with ornamental minarets at each corner and a main gate, with a magnificent main archway fashioned in the Islamic medieval style with twin minarets. Approach roads and walls were to be lined with palm trees for shade and for the eye's pleasure. Main buildings would be modern, functional affairs with arcaded facades, and you can see for yourselves that this is what happened.'

'Why did they do all that?' Ro asked.

'The purpose of this architectural throwback was to harmonise the concept of the historical caravanserai, or camel stop, with that of the modern truck stop or "kamyonserai" as I like to call them. That is to say; a 21st-century truck stop with a thirteenth-century theme. It was constructed during the 1990s and, as you can see, it wouldn't look out of place in Cairo, Istanbul, Damascus or Baghdad!'

Norman appeared and introductions were made. Norman, too, wanted to hear what this journalist had to say about the strange truck stop. Kamyonistan had been created by visionaries using pale-coloured materials, so that in the early mornings it appeared to float like a pearlescent city above the ground. Visionary, too, was the archway and the soaring minarets. Vision seemed to have evaporated, however, at ground level. Perhaps it was lack of money or dwindling enthusiasm; or maybe the visionaries' interest in the function of Kamyonistan ran out. Whatever the reason, the great compound, along with its neighbouring compounds, remained unmetalled. With no concrete or asphalt down, this spelt one certain thing in the Middle East: dust. It meant dust in summer and mud in winter. Kamyonistan, then, was a great dust bowl in the hills, surrounded by beautiful walls, gates and minarets. Its capacity was impressive. Before it opened, critics called it an Islamic theme park, accusing the architects of orientalist self-indulgence; and others registered alarm at its bold Islamic overtones. When the trucks began to roll in, however, there could be no mistaking its only possible function, casting aside any fantasies entertained by locals about a fortified village.

'I'd never heard of it before this trip,' Norman said.

'No one from Blighty had,' Eric replied. 'All the foreign wagons, as you know, are usually taken in an escorted convoy from the Turkish border at Bab al-Hawa to Homs truck stop, then to Damascus ring road, from where the Beirut convoy goes west and the rest are taken south to the Jordanian border at Naseeb.'

'Unless, like me, you bung the convoy official and do it all in one go by yourself!' Norman chuckled.

'Why didn't we come in a convoy?' Ro asked.

'They tried putting lorries bound for Kamyonistan in convoys, but gave up. If you're not transiting Syria but tipping here, there's not much point in you being in one. It's only recently that any imports have come from the UK to Kamyonistan,' Eric said. 'Last year they expanded the zone here, clothes manufacturers have moved in, and hanging garments are being driven to northern Europe.'

'I should think most of it goes on Turkish and Eastern bloc wagons, doesn't it?' Norman said.

'You're right; but British long-haulers always have a nose for movements that pay. The biggest attraction is that they can get a load both ways. What did you bring down, bolts of cloth?'

'No, machinery.'

'It's usually cloth, I'm told.'

'Trouble is,' Norman said, 'you can't just do Middle East work when you feel like it. The work needs to be reliable. You need to be geared up for it. You need permits, carnets, triptychs and everything.'

'Extra insurances!' Eric added. 'And the driver needs to know the ropes.'

'Yes,' Norman sighed, turning to Ro. 'If you think about it, a driver's got to be able to look after himself; be a banker, a diplomat…'

'An asset manager,' Eric put in. 'A loaded lorry can be worth a fortune.'

'A communicator,' Norman said.

'Bit of a linguist, too.'

'A mechanic.'

'A geographer.'

'A bureaucrat, a bookkeeper.'

'And on top of that, a skilful and adaptable driver!'

'And,' Ro added gleefully, 'be able to do cooking and laundry.'

'So now you know the history of Kamyonistan, Ro!' Norman laughed.

'Why's it called that? What does it mean?' Ro asked.

'Aha!' Eric said. 'It started as a nickname. The truck stop opened before the transport zone was built and the Turks bringing in building materials and supplies nicknamed it "Kamyonistan", which in Turkish means "Truckland". Eventually, the name became used for the whole zone, and the Syrians were using it, too. There's an official, boring name for it that roughly translates as North Damascus Transport Zone; but I do know that the restaurant has "Kamyonistan" on its headed notepaper and that the indigenous haulage outfit calls itself "Kamyonistan-TIR". You may have seen their seventies, double-drive "New Generation" Mercedes 1928s with big air-breathers running up the front offside edge of the cabs, pulling tilts about.'

'Come on,' Norman said. 'Let's help these lads back with their tackle. I can feel an Efes coming on.'

'Why not try Barada? It's Syrian.'

HGV-positive

The journalist and the drivers repaired to the bar. Meanwhile, discretion being the better part of sneakiness, Nuri and Ro betook themselves to a far corner of the compound where a couple of abandoned old trucks stood. A few Turkish lorries had escaped from the convoy and were snaking their way among the stationary wagons. The evening call to prayer sounded, and two Syrians in red and white *shamagh*s paused while the rubbish they were burning filled the air with acrid smoke.

Deep in the corner was a space where a truck had been, for there was debris there still. Next to this space the boys discovered an ancient Fiat 682 with a box trailer stationed beneath a palm tree. Its windscreen was opaque with dust and the dark red paintwork had turned matt. The rear axle was marooned on blocks, whilst the front one rested on Trilex wheels, which were slightly turned out and shod with deflated tyres. Much of the bodywork showed signs of rust. Parts had been messily removed, leaving wires trailing from gaping holes where headlamps, wipers and batteries had once been. An impressive roof rack sat on the cab, and was slightly skewed as if someone had given up trying to remove it. The number plate was Turkish and began with 31, indicating that it had been registered in Antakya, across the border; but the home-made metal sun visor displayed Arabic script.

Ro heaved the door open on the driver's side. To their surprise, it was clean inside and empty of any personal effects apart from a blanket folded on the bunk. Curtains were drawn across the windscreen. The two boys climbed in and nodded in tacit approval of the new hideaway. Ro swung onto the little bunk and lay with his hands behind his head. Nuri wafted the hot air out with the creaking door then sat on the bunk.

'Welcome to Hotel Fiat!' Ro said.

'Thank you!'

'Hey! Could we really make the camels carry water?' Ro asked.

'Yes, of course!' Nuri said.

'Would your grandfather let us try? I mean, if I helped you to put the saddles on and load them properly? They could carry the brushes, too.'

'I don't think he'll stop us,' Nuri said. 'Last night he was planning to make me charge drivers for rides, like tourists, because he needs to go to Saudi for a week or so to sort out a family problem. But I don't think drivers want camel rides. He knows that too, really.'

'No, they want their trucks washed,' Ro said.

'I'll ask him tonight. A camel-wash for lorries!'

Ro frowned. 'I don't think that miserable kid on his dad's truck-wash machine will be very pleased.'

'Don't worry about him!' Nuri said, launching himself onto Ro and tickling him with his one hand.

'Let's use this as our den,' said Ro. 'I'll get the spare gas stove, the little one, and some mugs. Maybe they'll let us sleep here.'

Nuri took Ro's hand and pulled him up. 'Let's go and ask now, about the camels and the lorry den.'

'Hotel Fiat, you mean.'

Ro was woken three times next morning; the first time by the dawn call to prayer, the second time by a cock crowing from somewhere in the direction of the restaurant, and the third time by his uncle trying to find the tea things with a hangover. Ro showered, breakfasted and ran across the TIR parking to find his friend, his *shamagh* fluttering in the breeze. Nuri's grandfather seemed enthusiastic about the idea. He was also keen to escape to Saudi sooner rather than later.

Nuri and his grandfather patiently taught Ro how to position and secure the saddle properly and how to make the camel kneel and stand. It was necessary to learn this thoroughly before setting off. With one arm, Nuri would be hard pushed to intervene if things went awry. It also became apparent to Ro that much of the lifting would fall to him simply because he had two arms. They tried to do everything together, however, so that Nuri could pass on his skills. So they practised loading one camel together and then tackled the other. With just a few five-litre containers they would last all day.

Finally, they set off, leading their beasts of burden. Their success was immediate because it was such a novelty. The Turkish drivers, in particular, were delighted by the idea. By midday they had washed trucks solidly and their arms ached. 'Let's get something to eat,' Nuri suggested. So they parked the camels by the restaurant and got a chicken kebab sandwich apiece and some freshly squeezed orange juice.

Returning to work, Ro noticed his camel's eyelashes because they were really long, like Nuri's, except that Nuri's were thick and flicked up at the ends. Nuri was in his element and looked blissfully contented. Ro was happy too, but he was still struggling to keep control of his camel. He knew it would be some time before he could relax with it.

By mid-afternoon they had washed another lorry and given camel rides to the peanut vendor and one of the shoeshine boys in exchange for a newspaper cone full of nuts. Then Eric discovered them and wanted pictures for his piece on Kamyonistan. 'This really completes the whole concept of the place,' he cried delightedly. He wanted to take pictures with some of the 'oldies' in the background. 'For a transport historian like me, Ro, the Middle East is an astonishing place. These older lorries are contemporaries of the wagons that came down here from England and the rest of Europe in the seventies and eighties. They've long vanished from the transport scene at home, but here they all are! It's like being in an open air working museum. Some of them, like that LS329 Mercedes over there, are from the early sixties.'

'How come they last so long here, then?'

'Lots of reasons, mate. Legislation's the main one: these wouldn't pass any kind of UK test. Then there's the cost of maintenance: no British haulier could afford to keep one of these on the road. Also, the mechanics in these little roadside work-shops think nothing of engineering a new part from bits of scrap, and that saves a fortune on fitting brand new parts. Round the back here you'll find boys no older than you two doing just that.

The weather too, accounts for a lot; much of the desert is hot and dry, so nothing rusts quickly. Then of course, there's the plain economic fact that many of these owner-drivers can't afford a newer model.'

'What's your favourite truck, then?' Nuri asked.

'Well, none of them really,' Eric replied. 'I'd want a hybrid tractor unit, taking my favourite attributes from various models. Let's see; I'd probably go for a DAF cab, a Scania engine and an Eaton gearbox.' Eric ducked as Nuri swung the camel's nose-rope over his head.

'You'll get run over in a minute,' Ro laughed. Ro loved the way the colours of his camel appeared to change, subtly, as it moved and caught the light. Already, he was developing affection for the strange creature.

'Just look at that, son!' Eric piped up.

'What's that?'

'That blue trailer.' An artic slowly undulated across the un-even ground.

'An old twelve-metre tilt,' Ro observed.

'Good boy! Yes, a forty-foot spread-axle tilt.'

'Why "spread-axle"?'

'Those old two-axle trailers – "tandem-axle", we called them – had to bear a lot of weight, so they placed the two axles far apart to spread that weight.'

'Why do the drivers call a hole in the ground a "spread-axle toilet", then?'

'Because you have to spread your axles to squat over them, of course!'

'It's got Arab writing on the side; what does it say, Nuri?'

'"Trans-Asia, Damascus,"' Nuri read.

Eric said, 'It's even got Trilex wheels, look. You can tell those by the big spokes.'

'Looks old-fashioned.'

'Does now, of course. No side bars or under-run bars, no spray suppressors. Beautiful trailer: poetry in motion.' Ro looked at him sideways. Then he watched the tilt's progress, as its chassis slowly twisted and untwisted over the bumps and the sheet tightened and slackened over its frame.

'A tilt is a living, breathing thing, Ro,' Eric murmured wistfully. 'It's not like other trailers at all.' They watched the double-drive Volvo F89 heading it grind to a halt with a hiss and a cloud of dust.

'Uncle Norman says the best sort of tilt is one you've just set fire to,' Ro said. 'He hates them.'

'He has no soul! It's probably the most versatile trailer ever invented,' Eric said, as the Volvo restarted and began to turn away. The tilt canopy rippled and flickered with flashes of gold in the setting sun, its grimy long-haul patina transformed for an instant from industrial to celestial.

'Uncle Norman reckons they're out of date and dangerous to work with, especially when it's wet,' Ro persisted.

'A tilt driver knows the weather by the way his trailer sways and shudders in its sleep,' Eric said. 'He knows, like the captain of a tall ship, how to park into, or out of wind, sun and rain to avoid unsheeting catastrophes during loading. His side boards will be carefully colour-coded with blobs of paint and marked with positional references to ensure efficient reassemblage.'

'You should get out more, Eric,' Ro remarked dryly.

'I do! You think I'm an anorak, don't you?'

'More like a cycling cape, I'd say.'

'You'll learn. It gets in your blood, all this. It never goes away. I'm afraid I suffer from *anoraksia verbosa* and I'm HGV-positive too! There's no hope for me.'

When Ro presented himself for dinner, the drivers were already well oiled. Eric was still in full flow about how drivers had a much more intimate relationship with a tilt than a fridge because of all the climbing about and rebuilding that went on.

'Eric!' Norman shouted, 'have you ever fallen off a tilt?'

'Well, no.'

'Try it, mate, most of us have! Perhaps it'll cure you. You're a derv addict without a wagon, mate. Isn't that so, Ro?'

'He's all right, Eric!' Ro protested. Everyone laughed.

'I suppose he's harmless enough,' Norman said.

Ro thought of tilts flexing and dilating in the moonlight and quickly made himself think of camels sitting munching hay by starlight instead. There was hope for him yet.

Overlanders

By the time the sun had risen high enough to fuse the time-honoured truck stop smells of diesel, urine, rubbish fires and outdoor cooking, the boys were washing their first lorry of the day. One camel sat and the other one stood patiently chewing regurgitated cud. Several drivers were 'running-up' their engines to keep the batteries interested.

They were just settling down to take *shay* with their host, when Nuri's grandfather appeared in his small truck. He was off to Saudi and he assured Nuri that he had stacked all the hay bales against Hotel Fiat and left some cooking things in the footwell of the unit.

'You told him about the den!' Ro later said accusingly.

'He was going to make me stay outside!' Nuri answered.

'I'll move in with you tonight,' Ro grinned.

Another arrival that morning was a rigid truck with a passenger body like a utility workmen's bus, with 'Overland Tours' painted on the front. They decided to wash it when they saw its English registration plates.

'We've just put in for repairs, lads,' the driver told them. 'We won't be hanging about for long.'

They washed it anyway. One of the overlanders was a retired schoolteacher in a cerise and violet cotton print dress and wide-brimmed straw hat who looked dressed for Sports Day. Her name was Titania Roberts. She explained to the boys that the overlanders were going from London to Khartoum and back, visiting everything possible on the way. She took a great interest in their little enterprise.

In the late afternoon Ro had his first driving lesson. After unsaddling the camels in their new corner of the compound and leaving Nuri to ensconce himself in the Fiat, Ro hurried back to Norman's ERF.

'I've dropped the trailer, so you can get to grips with the unit first,' Norman said. 'Gearbox is going to be the hard bit at first. Come on.' Soon the ERF was setting hesitantly off across the ground and out into the service road.

They arrived back an hour later to find a DAF 95 Super Space and tilt parked alongside Jumbo. It sported distinctive yellow Saudi transit plates fore and aft.

'Bingo's here!' Norman shouted. 'You'll like him. Bit of a one-off. Used to be a librarian, I think.' Like Titania Roberts, Bingo took an interest in the camel-wash and looked forward to meeting Nuri. He was on his way back from Doha in Qatar on the Arabian Gulf.

Ro collected a few useful kitchen items and went to find Nuri in Hotel Fiat. Nuri had found the keys under the driver's seat, so they now had a door key each.

'We should keep chickens,' Nuri said.

'Why?'

'Eggs!'

Ro hugged him. They put the kettle on and domestic bliss was established.

In the setting sun, Ro joined the throng of beer-swilling drivers again. 'I drove right round the zone,' he told Bingo, 'corners and everything! Plus, I can now double-declutch.'

'Don't be filthy!' Bingo retorted.

'He's a natural, mate,' Norman put in generously. 'I've seen it before in youngsters. I was the same, of course.' They laughed. 'His mum'd kill me if she were here. She wanted him to be a solicitor or something.' The sunset call to prayer started. 'What's that you've wrapped round your head, Ro?' Norman asked.

'It's the *shamagh*. You know, the one Nuri gave me.'

'Take it off.'

'Why? It keeps the dust out and the sun off. I like it.'

'You're English, Ro. You can't go round dressing up like a rag-head.' Norman reached into the cab and took a cap from the dashboard and tossed it in the boy's direction. 'You're English, mate!'

'So is that why you want me to wear an American baseball cap?' Ro flashed back pointedly.

'Have you any idea what you look like?'

'I don't feel silly. Anyway it was Nuri's, and he's my mate…'

'Why shouldn't Ro wear it?' Jumbo interjected. 'Who makes up these rules?'

'The old brigade, from the days of the Raj of course!' Bingo broke in good-humouredly. 'Never go native! Rots the brain! Erodes the culture. Norman's a product of colonialism.'

'Personally,' Jumbo said evenly, 'I've always found headgear extremely useful out here. Never be without one in a sandstorm! The old Bedu weren't daft when they came up with these tea towels. The trick is, never to wear them to the supermarket at home with the missus.' They laughed.

'That's as may be,' Norman said, trying a new tack, 'but he's wearing another boy's clothes.'

'Yeah! Like a friendship bracelet,' Ro tried.

'Bracelets are for poofters,' Norman said.

'I'll wear it as a scarf, then.'

'Wear it like a scarf and you'll look like a girlie. Wear it on your bonce and you'll look like a girlie. I'm trying to protect you, mate.'

'From?'

'Losing your culture; your identity.'

'He's not losing his identity,' Bingo said, 'he's adjusting it to accommodate part of another culture. Ro's engaging with that culture, and his own cultural identity will be more robust for it.'

'You can engage with the natives perfectly well without wearing their head-cloths,' Norman said stubbornly.

'You're a tribal fossil!' Bingo said. 'And the sun's gone down over the mirror arm. Come on, bar's open.'

'May I sleep out tonight?' Ro asked tentatively. Now or never, he thought. 'Nuri and I have made a camp in an old lorry so that we can keep an eye on the camels.'

Norman narrowed his eyes and locked the cab door. 'Keep your wits about you then and don't take anything valuable with you.'

Ro rewound his *shamagh* round his head and set off into the twilight.

One Foot in Paradise

The rattle and roar of the motor on a fridge trailer parked nearby woke Ro next morning. He saw that the door was open and wondered how Nuri had got up without disturbing him. Nuri was boiling the kettle over an open fire thrown together with scrap wood from packing cases and fanning the flames with the hem of his jalabiya. When challenged, he told Ro that it was saving gas. After breakfasting on tea, flat bread and oranges, they prepared the camels for a working day.

Their first customer's truck bore an oval country-of-origin sticker with 'UZ' on it. 'Uzbekistan,' the driver told them. His Mercedes SK was shod with oversize tyres that, according to the driver, he'd acquired in Iran. Squatting flat-heeled by the tilt, they drew lines in the dust to show their journeys. The driver wanted to know the route Ro had taken, and he was clearly excited about Paris and London. He conveyed to them that he was from Tashkent, the Uzbek capital. His journey home would take him through eastern Turkey, then Tehran in Iran, across Turkmenistan and then through Bokhara and Samarkand to Tashkent. They washed only the unit, before moving on.

Their next customer was Aziz. He was Syrian and drove an Arab-style Mercedes 1928 with a bonnet and a roof-mounted air-conditioning unit. His silver-painted, tandem-axle fridge trailer had a stack of leaf springs each side. 'For sixty-four tonnes,' Aziz told them. More drawing in the dust took place. 'First I go to Aqaba in Jordan,' he said. 'There I catch a ferry to Nuweiba in Egypt.' Nuri became excited; he knew Nuweiba Port. 'From there I go to Cairo, then up to the Mediterranean and into Libya. From Tripoli I catch a slow ferry that calls in at all the Med ports and finally puts in at Tangier in Morocco. Then I go south through Casablanca and Marrakech and climb right over the top of the High Atlas Mountains at Tizi n' Tichka. It is the highest road pass in Morocco. I have to grind up hours of narrow, steep hairpin bends through fantastic scenery on the road up from Marrakech. Then more of the same on the southern descent into the rocky Sahara and on to Ouazarzate. It is tough work with a full-sized lorry like this. At the top of the pass there is only room for a handful of lorries to park, but the little huddle of restaurants and shops are worth stopping for.' Ro was amazed at such journeys.

By the time the camel-wash boys were heading to the restaurant for lunch, they had also encountered an Iranian with a Volvo F10 double-drive unit on big tyres, who had just brought in a load from Moscow via the Black Sea.

They had become really fired up about these epic journeys and wanted to tell Norman about them. He wasn't in the restaurant, but Bingo was. Bingo was having a nice quiet conversation with Titania Roberts, the retired teacher. They were both sixty and had immediately taken a liking to each other's company. Bingo stood up and led them to a big wall map where, with much animated finger thrusting, the boys traced the routes of their customers.

'He was even more excited about us going to Paris than we were about Samarkand!' Ro said.

'That's what I like about this work,' Bingo said. 'Now look, here's Doha where I've just come from.' They followed his finger along the route across Saudi and Jordan to Syria.

During their lunch, Titania said, 'These journeys are geographical ones. Your driver had come from Uzbekistan, Aziz was off to southern Morocco and your journey is from England; but what about your other journey?'

'Other journey?'

'The one you make inside. Part of your mind is learning about the places you travel through. Another part of your mind is making a different journey in which you learn about yourself as you go… Pass me that tabbouleh, will you?'

'Like a sort of shadow?' Ro ventured.

'Exactly! A shadow journey.'

'How do I know the difference?'

'When your journey changes your behaviour and shows you how to make changes to yourself, you know that's the shadow one.'

'Nuri is making me more tolerant of people who don't understand much English,' Ro volunteered.

'Yes, and your relationship with Nuri is probably showing you much more than tolerance. You're learning how to cherish someone; I can see that. It's all part of your shadow journey.'

Nuri looked at Titania and said, 'I know this shadow journey. It made me strong on camel treks when my side was healing.' He sat back and munched his falafel.

'Couldn't you just have the shadow journey and not do the real one?' Ro asked.

'Maybe,' Titania replied, 'but I suspect that people with itchy feet and wanderlust need their actual journey as a sort of framework for the shadow journey.'

'And you? Are you making a shadow journey?'

'Yes,' Titania replied, 'I am. Mine is helping me to come to terms with retirement after a lifetime's dedication to teaching. It will be a long journey, which is why I booked a trip to Khartoum!'

Nuri turned to Bingo. 'What about you?' he challenged. 'What have journeys taught you?'

'Well, for a start, they've taught me how to be,' Bingo answered.

'To be what?' Ro asked.

'When I started driving I was a human *doing*, always having to be active and finding things to keep me busy. I learned that "doing" is not necessarily productive and that "being" is not necessarily complacent. Driving taught me to be a human *being*, because there is so much unavoidable delay – waiting for customs, for loads and so on, that you just have to learn to sit and watch the world and accept that fact. You lose both the urge to keep doing things and the guilt that keeps you doing them.'

'Now that's just the sort of journey I need to make!' Titania exclaimed. 'You must teach me. But first of all I want to see these boys' camels.'

On the way out, Titania noticed the sign above the entrance and asked Nuri what it meant. 'It says *Matam Janna*. It means "Paradise Restaurant". *Janna* is paradise.'

'This must be a sort of paradise for you boys,' Titania laughed.

'Paradise is after we're dead,' Nuri said.

'Paradise is inside our heads,' Ro said.

'Whoa!' Bingo cried. 'That's three different paradises. Four, if you count the restaurant.'

'I say!' Titania said. 'Let's meet here tomorrow for lunch with our own ideas about paradise and compare them.'

'Typical teacher!' Bingo laughed. 'But I quite like it. I'll see if some of the others will play. Eric will, I know.'

'To the paradise club!' said Titania, raising an imaginary glass, as Bingo left them.

The sun glared brassily on the remaining trio as they moved among the camels. 'I've got an idea,' Titania said. 'If you don't mind, that is.'

'Go on,' Ro prompted.

'When I have to think about something and I'm not sure about it, I always ask God to give me a clue. Then I empty my mind and something always pops in.'

'We could give it a try,' Ro said dubiously.

'Even better, we could go in the drivers' mosque and do it there. The atmosphere'd be better,' Titania said. 'What about it, Nuri? OK, you're in charge! We'll take our shoes off at the door, don't worry.'

They led the camels to the mosque, which stood on the edge of the compound, and settled them. Then they filed in quietly. It was a lovely cool, light, airy place and nobody was about. Padding across the carpets in bare feet, they sat down near the centre and took deep breaths. Intense maroons and golds shone where the sun fell upon the carpets. Outside, they could hear birdsong and distant diesels. They luxuriated in the stillness. Ro sat a little to one side, just behind Nuri, who was kneeling. Nuri's perfectly formed ears were protruding at an exquisite angle against the shafts of sunlight.

'I feel serene,' Ro said.

'I feel smiley,' Nuri said.

'I feel contented,' Titania said. 'But is it paradise?'

'I don't see why not,' Ro said.

'I think you have to feel these things unconsciously if they are to count as paradise,' Titania said.

'I see what you mean. As soon as you are knowing, it sort of fades away,' Ro said.

'Step into the fairy ring and the fairies disappear!' Titania added.

'All right,' Ro said. 'How do you create happiness that isn't set up consciously?'

'You don't. It creates itself, if you let it.'

'That's a bit mysterious. I want to be able to switch it on and off.'

A cloud dimmed the mosque's natural light. All the intensity faded from the carpets. Then suddenly, light was restored in all its brilliance as the cloud passed.

'That's what paradise is like!' Nuri shouted. 'It comes and goes.'

'It's in the space between the clouds!' Ro grinned.

'Paradise intermittent!' Titania exclaimed.

Ro wanted to reach out and touch his friend's ears, but he knew it would be inappropriate. Then he fondled Nuri's ears anyway and Nuri looked at him in astonishment. He then got the giggles. Paradise was like that.

They found Eric minding the camels when they emerged into the brightness. He nodded at the horizon and said, 'I'm not happy with that sky. Now, tell me about this paradise business…'

'We'll do one more wash, shall we?' Ro suggested. They roused the dozing beasts. Eric escorted Titania away.

'I reckon Eric thinks this place is paradise,' Ro said. Nuri laughed and started singing.

A weary contingent of lorry washers plodded across the great parking compound at close of day. Little bursts of dust enclouded their camels' footfalls and hung with tender Beduin singing in the gloaming. Leading his beast of burden, the singer, wearing his headgear in that soft and careless way that boys so often do, flashed a grin at Ro. They'd done well today, and Nuri was feeling triumphant. His camel momentarily lost its footing and protested with hoarse hooting and much dramatic casting about. A heavy, unmistakable camel odour assailed them briefly. Ro drew alongside, leading his camel with encouraging clicks, while in the distance the sound of a diesel engine was extinguished, to be replaced immediately by the evening call to prayer from the mosque. Another took up the cry, and their waves of chant overlapped then echoed from the walls and buildings. Drivers sat quietly between the trucks, smoking or heating their *shay* kettles.

'Tomorrow,' Nuri said, 'we'll be rich.'

'Tomorrow?' Ro murmured, as if struggling with the concept. He'd forgotten about the future; England's rain and GCSEs. For the moment, paradise was in the present. He said, 'Tomorrow, I think I'm having a driving lesson.'

When the mosques fell silent, Nuri resumed his contented singing, and they made for their corner.

Ro was torn between sustaining the camel magic and driving the ERF in the morning. Were the camels a greater bond between Nuri and him than the trucks were? he wondered. Without the trucks there'd be no camels, he decided, so it must be both; in which case he could do both tomorrow. 'We'll have to diesel-up these camels before we turn in,' he told Nuri, who continued to sing in the dwindling light.

Janna

Ro suffered from a gurgling stomach in the night and ran a slight temperature. Deliriously, the thoughts and ideas of paradise fragmented in his head like the little shapes in a kaleidoscope. He found himself at the wheel of the lorry on a shining causeway, which was suspended in a midnight blue sky with bright stars. With him on the causeway were pearly-white wagons trailing filmy light behind them. Far ahead was Kamyonistan, with light streaming from its walls and minarets. A boy wearing a white *shamagh* pulled up alongside him in another lorry. He called out to Ro. It was Nuri, and he was laughing in that contagious way of his.

'Where are we going, Nuri?'

'Kamyonistan, Ro! There is another place! *Yallah*, let's go, *yallah!*' Nuri was breathless with joy and he surged ahead. Ro's truck didn't seem to be making any progress.

'Don't leave me, Nuri,' he said, panicking. 'Please don't leave me!' He was overcome with a desperate sensation of loss, separation and abandonment. Then he awoke suddenly. A camel coughed. Behind the compound wall, a lorry with a chronic gearbox whine accelerated up the service road. Nuri's even breathing sounded softly in his ear, and Ro drifted peacefully back to sleep.

The Paradise Club

A din woke Ro. At first he couldn't work out what it was. The light was subdued. Ro turned to Nuri, whose brown eyes shone into his. Rain. It rattled on the metal roof; it felt as though they were tucked up inside a drum. Then Nuri leapt out of bed. 'The feed!' he shouted. In the pouring rain the two boys stowed bales of hay underneath the old trailer.

In just a few hours, the compound had become a sea of mud. It caked the wheels of lorries, it clouded puddles, it stained the hems of jalabiyas and sullied the restaurant floor. Restaurant Janna was packed with drivers, agents, vendors and officials drinking *shay* to keep out of the rain.

The boys found Eric who knew where the others were. The noise was deafening: loud Arab music, loud voices, loud crockery. 'Let's go on the veranda!' Bingo shouted, 'it's quieter.'

Despite the rain, the air was warm and one by one the Paradise Club members appeared on the veranda. They pushed two tables together.

'With your permission,' Titania announced, taking the chair automatically, 'we'll conduct this like a sort of debate. No rules, but each takes a turn at explaining "paradise". If we want a vote at the end, all well and good. If it's not necessary, we needn't. OK?'

'Hardly a day for debating paradise!' Norman grumbled. The overlanders' driver appeared with a large tray of tea, before setting off to the workshops, where his truck was over an inspection pit. The other tourists had taken taxis into Damascus. Ramazan came out with a tray piled with flatbread, olives and lots of boiled eggs, at Bingo's thoughtful behest.

'Right, gentlemen!' Titania said. 'Where is paradise?'

'You start!' Bingo cried. 'You should set us an example!'

'Well,' Titania replied, 'I haven't given it much thought. I'd rather intended just to chair the meeting. I reckon the ancient

Greeks and Romans had the monopoly of paradise locations. You could work your way round the Med and stop only at sites like Delphi and Cyrene. I suppose that's what we overlanders are really, paradise tourists. I sometimes look up and see a gold-laced cloudscape and it evokes my childhood notion of heaven. Is paradise up there in that glorious place? Well, no, I've been up in an aeroplane and looked down on those sun-shot castles of cloud and – surprise, surprise! There is no paradise; only within. All I ask for, really, is that feeling of paradise inside me, along with running water, competent midwives and the certainty of a gin and tonic among the delphiniums at sunset. And perhaps the odd centurion on chilly nights.'

'Well said!' Bingo laughed. 'Who's next?'

'I'll go,' Norman said hesitantly. 'I know this paradise thing well. It comes upon me as I haul in low gear over the crest of a mountain road at the end of the day. I'm filled with a sense of paradise as the sun sets straight ahead beyond the distant hills which softly repeat in violet, indigo and lilac into the dusk…'

'Blimey!' Jumbo interrupted, 'Have you been at the *vino collapso* already?'

'Hush!' Bingo said firmly. 'This is not the time to dumb down a driver's thoughts – that's an English disease, I'm afraid!'

'Paradise for me,' Norman continued, 'is in the moment. Paradise for me is being absorbed in something I'm good at and enjoy doing. Perhaps I'm easily satisfied. I live for my work. Work is not a by-product, like it is for those drivers who work to live and who want to be home by teatime. Like all addictions – and you all know I like a drink – my kind of workaholism has its silver lining. When I'm not just a diesel junkie going through the motions, I'm a fully paid-up card-carrying member of paradise bowling along with the serenity of a man in perfect harmony with his wagon.'

Jumbo clapped and they all joined in. There was a general scrum for the olives and eggs.

'I'll go next, if you want,' Kees said. 'And I can include Nuri, too. I know he's a Muslim and must believe in paradise in the afterlife; but I hear that he also made an interesting observation about the intermittent nature of paradise as we experience it on earth. Is that all right, Nuri?' Nuri nodded and smiled. 'OK. Well, if paradise is intermittent, this accounts for its elusiveness. As Ro here put it, paradise appears to exist between the cloudy spells. This struck me one evening, years ago, driving down from Aleppo to Damascus. A fierce thunderstorm was rendering driving conditions intolerable; but between oppressive bouts the sun would reappear and send shafts of filtered light to strike the backs of roadside sheep with incandescent whiteness.'

'Oh-ho!' Titania exclaimed. 'Surely this was the very paradise in the minds of Victorian biblical painters, replete with all the imagery of tempest, flock and celestial light – not to mention the road to Damascus!'

'Ah! But this was no spiritual awakening, despite the rainbow haloes cast up before me by the spray from Turkish artics overtaking at lunatic speeds! Nonetheless, those luminous sheep serve to remind us how intermittent paradise can be.'

'Then perhaps,' Eric put in, 'it was merely ovine refulgence that blinded Paul on the road to Damascus.' There was laughter; then, more eating. Bingo called for a new tray of *shay*.

Ro started a slow handclap and chanted, 'Eric! Eric! Eric!' Eric held up both hands for silence.

'I know Ro here thinks that Kamyonistan is paradise for me, and I won't disappoint him. The advantage of locating paradise in a truck stop is that such places are an integral part of journeys. Journeys give meaning to the concept of truck stops. Our geographical journeys and our inner journeys are interwoven. For example, the first part of my inner journey from restless journalist to contented man of the road was inextricably bound with a difficult and adventurous lorry trip to Turkey in winter. Truck stops punctuate these journeys. Lives are made and broken here, along with the journeys. Some drivers resting at Londra Camp TIR park in Istanbul, for example, have revived themselves for the onward push into the orient. Others have bottled out, abandoned their trucks and flown home. The magic of Kamyonistan, here, is that it is not a destination for most of us, it's on the way to one. The element I'm interested in lies at the interface of the resting place and the epic journey. The relation-ship between a truck stop and the journeys made to and from it is at once dynamic and static; the journey moves, the truck stop doesn't. The journey is active; the truck stop is passive. A corner of paradise may lurk at that interface of being on a journey and not being on a journey. It's a euphoric state of mind. It is that sense of contented equilibrium attained by long-haul drivers at the exact interface of their journey and their resting place. I call it *kamyuforya*! It is probably true to say that although alcohol can temporarily enhance this natural sense of well-being, it is quick to blunt the experience.'

'That was good until the last bit!' Norman said.

'Eric?' Ro piped up mischievously. 'Do lorries go to paradise?'

'Of course they do,' Eric replied immediately, 'which is more than can be said of some of their drivers!'

Norman stood up. 'I need a beer,' he said. 'Can I get anyone else one while I'm up on my hind legs?'

'I'll have a large one!' Ro said.

'You two lads don't need alcohol to be happy,' Eric said, 'you're already bombed-out on childhood!'

'Wow!' Bingo said. 'That's the theme of my paradise contribution, coming up after the break!' There was a flicker of lightning and a crash of thunder. Nuri clutched Ro.

The rain stopped and the sun broke through. Norman returned clutching cans.

'I'm going for "paradise lost",' Bingo said when all was quiet. 'I think paradise is located in childhood. If you think about it, the paradise of myths, religions, legends and fairy tales is populated with children in the guise of angels, elves and fairies. This notion is tucked away in culture. Then we leave childhood – and with it, paradise. Jam yesterday, then! If we believe in the hereafter promised by religion, we can locate paradise in the future, when we're dead. Jam tomorrow, then! But I believe we can have "paradise present" if only we can recover our child selves in adulthood and maintain access to paradise into old age.'

'Call me a sceptic,' Titania interrupted, 'but anyone who is nostalgic for childhood has obviously never been a child.' They laughed.

'Childhood,' Bingo answered, 'is not necessarily a safe place to be, granted. Paradise is located in our child past; but that childhood doesn't equal paradise. Paradise, I reckon, exists in childhood as an unsustained thing. It's intermittent, as Kees so beautifully demonstrated.'

'So what about this child self you want to recover?' Titania asked. 'Are you talking about all those mental and emotional snapshots of ourselves not having our needs met aged two, five, twelve and fifteen?'

'No, I don't mean all those needy spectres. I mean the sum total of them and more. I mean the single distillation that is the spirit of our childhood; the inextinguishable little light that shines inside us and remembers who we once were. If we can take that into adulthood with us, we might get jam today. The hard bit has to be recovering the child self. One of the possible ways of doing this is to maintain our sense of an inner child by remembering who we were through observation of our own children. The shrinks have other methods of reconnecting us with the past. But to get back to paradise: unless we can find a way of carrying it with us over the threshold into adulthood, we leave it behind in childhood. Subsequent unhappiness is then rooted in the fear that we can never find our way back to recover what was so precious to us.' Bingo leaned forward. 'There's nothing necessarily wishy-washy, ethereal or even mysterious about the idea of a child self or child spirit. We carry the general concept of our past child with us in memories, sensations, ideas, impressions and the observations of others. Our ex-child is historical fact. Encoded within that total impression of our inner child is the magical sense of innocence, hope, optimism and openness that enabled us to receive paradise and to slip so effortlessly and imperceptibly in and out of it during childhood. It's up to us to choose to rediscover this most precious guiding light.'

Jumbo cracked open another can and spoke up. 'I don't want a proper turn, but I'll have my say. Firstly, this isn't paradise. It's a dirty, smelly, dusty hole full of horrible trucks in the middle of nowhere. How can a dump like this be paradise? Secondly, I believe in paradise in the hereafter, mate. It's too beguiling to ignore. Almond-eyed houris too, I hear. But when I meet the terminally ill, I have to strongly resist the temptation to ask them to remember me to Mum when they get to paradise! I see no either/or here. We can have this cake and eat it, claim paradise on earth as it is in heaven, and then have a second bite of the cherry when we die. That way, you get delayed gratification too, if it's the almond-eyed houris you're after. Mind you, if I was one of those jihadist types, I'd strap myself to almond-eyed houris first and leave the Semtex till later. They're all arse about face, if you ask me.'

'But do you really believe in paradise after death?' Bingo laughed.

'Yes, mate. I don't know how you can be any surer that paradise doesn't exist after death, than I can be sure that it does!'

'Fair comment.'

'I'm happy to put up with "jam tomorrow". That's what keeps me going; gives me something to believe in.'

'The "opium of the masses", as Marx would say.'

'Probably more effective than real opium! It isn't a brilliant analogy; most analogies aren't. Belief is better than opium.' Jumbo hiccupped, and they all laughed again.

Bingo said, 'It is possible that these primitive beliefs about the afterlife, instilled in kids, may help them to sustain their youthful optimism into old age.'

'Primitive?'

'Of course. It is a brilliant psychological device from ancient times and it probably stopped cavemen from jumping off cliffs on dark, winter nights. It's another fairy tale.'

'So there's no afterlife, then? I'd better get a life! Quick, pass me another beer!' There was a distant rumble of thunder. Jumbo glanced heavenwards. 'Only joking, mate!' he shouted.

The Paradise Club applauded. They looked out across the muddy lorries, where sunlight streamed from the palm fronds like wet silver.

'Do you want to say something, boys?' Titania asked.

Nuri shook his head. Ro said shyly, 'I had a dream in the night that paradise is Kamyonistan. But I couldn't get to it...' He shrugged. Everyone laughed.

'I declare the meeting over,' Titania announced.

In the afternoon the rain returned and drummed afresh on the Fiat's cab roof, drowning out the murmurs and sighs of the boys within. What did grown-ups know of paradise?

Lorries of Arabia

The next day was fine. Ro and Nuri had plenty of dirty lorries to wash. Eric appeared, wearing a black and white *shamagh*. 'Look out!' Ro shouted, 'here comes "Lorries of Arabia"!'

'I've come to shadow you, if you don't mind,' Eric said. 'You seem to have better luck than me when interviewing drivers.' Ro handed him a sponge. 'Where was Uncle Norman going? I saw his unit leave earlier.'

'To pick up the trailer. The locker's ready. He said he was going to park up next to your den so you could give it a really good wash before loading.'

'He probably wants to keep an eye on us,' Ro said sulkily.

'Kees is loading today. He's off in the morning. He's tipping in Manchester, Thursday week,' Eric said. Eric was useful because he could reach high up the trailers with the long brush. 'We'd better buy our own if Kees is leaving,' Ro said, finishing off a cab door.

Eric had had enough by midday and didn't do the afternoon shift. 'Have a look in the other compound, where the pumps and truck-wash are,' he said. 'There's an F-type Mack Aerodyne there that might want washing.' So they went there.

Nuri took the camels to a standing tap whilst Ro lounged against the defunct truck-wash kicking at the dust. A big youth approached. Ro recognised Mahmout, the truck-wash operator's son. He looked about sixteen or seventeen, tall and muscly; unlike Ro, who was more of a pipe-stem model. Mahmout was wearing a dirty white T-shirt and the red shorts. Marching right up to Ro, he took hold of Ro's shirt lapels with both hands. 'You stop truck-wash,' he snarled menacingly. 'We do truck-wash, not you!'

'Let go!' yelled Ro, struggling. 'Let go!'

Mahmout tripped him and fastened him to the gritty ground. Ro squirmed, but the big boy was sitting on his chest and holding his wrists to the earth. Ro could feel the heat of two dark knees beside his ears; he even observed the black hairs running up and down his assailant's powerful thighs. Mahmout slid further up Ro's chest so that his shorts nearly touched Ro's nose. Ro's anger and fear were placed on hold while he speculated about what might happen next and his possible means of escape.

He heard a thud. Suddenly Mahmout was on his feet, holding the side of his head. Nuri was standing there, and he had a second stone in his hand. Mahmout could see that Nuri meant business, but to retrieve his dignity he repeated his warning to stop the truck-washing enterprise. Unexpectedly, Mahmout sat down. He was bleeding. Instinctively, Ro fetched water from the camel and, using his shirt hem, he dabbed at his adversary's head. 'Perhaps he can help us, Nuri. We could cut him in. He'll keep attacking us if we leave him out.'

'What can he do?'

'He's tall. We could do with someone tall to reach up the trailer sides. Like Eric did.' Nuri looked sullen and his face betrayed a reluctance to give in to intimidation. He turned and led his camel away. 'Thanks, Nuri!' Ro called, 'for rescuing me, I mean.'

'We'll try him out!' Nuri replied without looking round.

Mahmout was, indeed, a capable assistant, who could comfortably reach the upper areas of the F-type Mack's trailer. However, true to his indolent nature, he soon tired and gave up. After just one truck, he left them alone. They went home early to find that Norman had slotted the Long-Haul Services tilt with its new locker into the corner place, underneath the tall minaret next to Hotel Fiat. The unit was standing a few feet in front. Ro and Nuri unloaded the camels and that evening Norman took Ro for another driving lesson.

'Feed the steering wheel from hand to hand, Ro,' Norman said as they turned into the road. 'Now watch this speed ramp, it's a young mountain! Drop a gear. Good. Now depress the clutch as you ride over the ramp, to protect the drive train. Right, now give it some welly.'

At the far end of the road they heard a loud hissing noise. Ro pulled up at the kerb. They climbed out and Norman slid underneath on his back. 'It's only an air hose come adrift,' he said. 'We'll have to walk back and get some spanners from the trailer locker.'

By the time they had found the right tools and a spare length of hose, Norman was overheating and in need of a restorative beer. So a detour was made to the bar. It was already full of people. Evening sunlight slanted in through the windows, penetrating blue layers of smoke and setting ablaze the glasses of amber *shay*. Jumbo was saying, 'There's four of us coming back to Tangier from Casablanca. We'd all been drinking in the Seamen's Mission there, so we were a bit delicate. Anyway, Roger comes on the CB. "What's another word for tight – four letters?"'

'Which Roger was that, mate?'

'Cornish Roger. But he's doing a flaming crossword, isn't he, on his steering wheel! Well, that kept us occupied all the way to Tangier.'

'Blimey, it must have been a hard crossword; it's a long way…'

'No! He had a whole book of them. Hello, here's Norman. Wanna beer, mate?'

Titania was in conversation with Bingo. Bingo turned to Ramazan, who had brought a tray of beers. 'You've got that old Arab music turned up a bit loud tonight!' Bingo shouted.

'It's not Arabic, it's Turkish. This is my cassette, this one.' He sang along with it, *'Deli gibi severem, seni ben*: I love you like crazy…!' Ramazan swung off to another table.

Bingo said, 'Wouldn't it be good if we could invent a drug which induced that sunny, childlike state of paradisal innocence.'

'Fairy dust'd be better,' Titania said. 'Just a sprinkle. No fuss, no needles, no pills, no bottles. Just a twinkling haze of fairy dust – and *pow*!'

'Twinkling haze?'

'Well, a violet twinkling haze, actually. It'd be like stepping into the fairy ring and the fairies don't disappear.'

'Brilliant!'

'Once in a blue moon, that happens to teachers, you know. You and the kids become so absorbed in some activity or piece of music, that for a brief moment they forget you're not a child at precisely that same moment that you do too,' Titania said.

'Would the dust affect the children, do you think?'

'Probably not. But what would become of the real children while their carers were in a childlike state under the influence of fairy dust? It'd be worse than alcohol!'

'They'd be abandoned!' Bingo said. 'A powerful sense of homecoming like that would prove to be highly addictive to adults, I reckon. You'd have to rehabilitate them by teaching them to find that sense of homecoming without the dust.'

'Square one, then. The sense of homecoming is paradise regained. Jam today.'

'We need to talk more about the relationship between paradise and homecoming, I think.'

Their meals arrived. Kees came in.

'Are you loaded, then, Kees?' Norman asked.

'Yes. Have you heard about the gassing?'

'Oh, no! Who?' Jumbo asked.

'Four Turks were gassed in their cabs, through the ventilation ducts. Wallets taken.'

'Thieving ratbags!'

'No, listen. This wasn't ordinary gas. It paralysed them, so that they were aware of everything, but powerless.'

'You're joking?'

'I'm not. One of the Turks saw the writing on the side of a trailer that pulled out straight afterwards. It was Czech.'

'Why am I surprised at that?' Jumbo cried.

'There's worse,' Kees went on. 'One of the Turks is dead. Heart attack – from the gas, they think.'

'Trouble is,' Eric said, 'after the Soviet Union broke up, vast quantities of unguarded weaponry fell into criminal hands. It was probably some nerve gas that no one knows anything about.'

'Have they caught them?'

'Yes, two of them. They're in police custody.'

'Good! You never know who's driving lorries these days. Take the people of the Balkans. Only recently they were running round the hills killing and maiming each other, now they're calmly driving trucks round Europe. Think about that.'

Ro ate lots. Nuri ate more. Jumbo drank lots. Norman drank more. It was quite late when Ro said, 'If there are baddies out there gassing people, shouldn't you get the unit?'

Norman staggered to his feet. 'Come on,' he said. It was dark, but the moon and a few street lights helped them to find the ERF. Ro took the torch lamp from under the bunk and held it while Norman scrabbled about under the cab. It took him twice as long to effect a repair because he kept dropping things and swearing. Finally, Norman wiped the grease off his hands and fired up the engine. The road was empty, and Norman drove at a steady pace, sounding off about the kind of criminals who end up driving wagons. He shouted, 'Even in England, we've…'

'The ramp!' Ro yelled. But it was too late. The tractor unit smashed into the speed ramp; the steering wheel spun and the lorry veered to the right. There was a terrible grinding noise underneath, and with a sickening lurch, it fell over to one side in the drainage ditch and stopped.

'Are you all right, Ro?'

'I think so. You?'

'My arm hurts. I nearly went through the roof!'

'We'd better get help.'

'We're lucky not to be badly injured. We could have hit one of these palm trees,' Norman muttered ruefully.

The pair walked back to the compound. That night Norman slept in Kees's wagon. It could all wait until morning.

TIR-stained and Dusty

At eleven next day, a group of drivers stood at the concrete edge of the drainage ditch. Resting at the top of it, but still attached to an elderly Syrian breakdown wagon, was the troubled ERF. Kees handed cigarettes to the Syrian crew while Norman hovered, his arm in a sling. A couple of mechanics crawled about underneath. 'Good job you weren't loaded,' Jumbo grunted.

Norman sighed and said, 'It'll cost more than the damned thing's worth to put this lot right, even out here.' The sump was smashed, both axles were damaged and possible gearbox damage was being diagnosed. The freight agent, whom they'd borrowed to interpret for them said, 'They want to know if they must take it to the workshop.'

'No.' Norman shook his head. 'I'll be skint after paying for the recovery. Tell them to shove it under the trailer. It's in the corner. At least that way no one can nick the trailer.'

'What are you going to do?' Jumbo asked.

'Fly home and raise some funds. An old mate of mine's got a lovely Magnum he's getting shot of. He'll let me pay him, as and when. I could bring an old trailer down and flog it when I'm tipped.'

'Come back with me!' Kees said. 'I'm loaded and ready to go. We can double-man it back to Manchester.'

'What about Ro?' Norman asked.

'I can stay here,' Ro said.

'Don't be daft, you can't do that!'

'Why not? I want to. I've got the camel-wash. And I can keep an eye on the lorry. Live in it, even. Anyway, Nuri can't do it on his own.'

Norman flicked open a cab locker and produced a clutch of cans. Handing them round to those who wanted beer, he took a deep breath and said, 'You're a gentleman, Kees. Let's go for it;

though I'm not sure how much driving I can do with this arm.'

'No problem! That Stralis is an automatic. You can't wriggle out of it that easily!'

By early afternoon, the ERF had been pushed into place under its trailer; Ro had been given a small contingency fund in sterling; Norman had departed with Kees; and the boys were already moving into the more spacious 'Hotel Long-Haul'.

First they stacked broken pallets against the rear of the trailer for steps. Then they stacked all the camel feed inside, against the headboard and carried their kitchen gear in to create a dining area. Lastly they placed the saddles and the long-handled brushes donated by Kees on the tailboard for easy access. The neighbouring wrecks were positioned further forward than Hotel Long-Haul, so it was partially hidden from view, deep in the corner. Enjoying their sunny, secluded spot, they sat in garden chairs in front of the unit for a full two minutes before realising that they hadn't eaten.

While Nuri went foraging for food, Ro sat and pondered. His one-armed, lightning-struck, teenage Beduin cameleer had brought a considerable quantity of sunshine into his life. He was conscious of this and was able to express his thanks to the universe, to God or to fate – he wasn't sure which – through his friendship, the daily bonding of which was daily facilitated by the camel-wash enterprise. If Ro's feeling of well-being was his profit, then he was happy to plough it back into the business of living with Nuri; back into the already rich soil of their companionship. As each hour passed, the notion of life without Nuri had become less conceivable. Because their mutual regard had increased commensurately with their physical, attraction to one another, they were not particularly inclined to question their happy explorations of sunny intimacy. The natural innocence of this alliance prevailed against their shadowy notions of adult disapproval. He loved Nuri's pureness of spirit and above all, he loved his limitless sweetness, wherein lay both Nuri's strength and his vulnerability.

They watched the coming and going of wagons from far-off lands. It stimulated their sense of wanderlust to see place names written on the sides of them: Oslo, Dubai, Bucharest, Kuwait,

Athens and Madrid. Ro fingered the pages of his passport and Nuri sighed. 'Where would you like to go, Nuri?'

'Nuweiba, on Sinai. There's a port there, where all the lorries line up for the ferry to Aqaba in Jordan. It's a Beduin town. I could make a camel-wash there and be near to my family.'

'Good plan! What's it like?'

'Beautiful. You can swim in the Red Sea and ride your camel along the beach at sunset. Always warm and peaceful.'

'Except for the lorries.'

'They queue up in the main street. Perfect for a camel-wash. And everyone's used to camels in Nuweiba. There are lots of them there.'

Ro imagined Nuri climbing the front of a Mercedes in Nuweiba, trying to balance while struggling with a long brush. He frowned. But of course, he'd be there too, to support Nuri, wouldn't he? 'Would you go to Nuweiba without me, Nuri?'

Nuri looked staggered. 'Of course not!' He put his hand in Ro's and asked, 'Where do you want to go, Ro?'

Istanbul, Doha and Tripoli flashed through Ro's mind. 'Wherever you go, Nuri,' he said firmly.

A horn blasted in the distance. They recognised the yellow four-wheel-drive MAN belonging to the overlanders, as it bounced towards the grand exit and to Khartoum. 'Titania was nice.' Nuri commented.

'Yes,' Ro said. 'I'll miss her.'

Titania Roberts was beginning to suffer from overexposure to the constant barrage of drivers' tales. She had felt as if she had driven 10,000 kilometres by bedtime. Then she'd dreamt about her teaching days… 'Stand, girls, please! Good morning, everyone. Good morning, Gemma, even. Thank you. All right, girls, sit down and do not start talking. Now, have you all put your tachographs in? Alison I can see yours on your desk, dear. Put it in and set it for "drive": little picture of a steering wheel, that's it. OK, has everyone checked her oil and water this morning? Kicked her tyres, even the trailer ones? Good. Now, homework: there are only fourteen sets of CMR notes in the tray. Every set in by playtime, please, or you'll be tri-stacking flatbed trailers in the yard at lunchtime. Yes Angela, you can give me your TIR carnet instead. That was a nice little run down to Istanbul for you, wasn't it? You can take your hijab off now though. Talking of which, while I call the register, girls, you'd better see that you've got a full uniform on today. There'll be an inspection going into assembly, so make sure that you have your hi-vis vests on. Karen, where are your steel-capped boots? Lend her a pair, someone. Where's Sally-Ann this morning? Having her eleven-hour break? But girls, she only drove six hours with a twelve-hour spread-over yesterday; and she forgot to diesel up before parking. OK, now listen for your names on the register. Palm couplings? Bottom drawer, dear. Daphne, put your trailer legs down and sit properly...'

A sonorous call to prayer floated across the TIR park and reminded them that the afternoon was growing old. Nuri decided to perform his prayers and, spreading out his *shamagh* as a prayer mat, he seized a water container and began his ablutions.

'Show me,' Ro said. 'I want to do them, too.'

So Nuri taught Ro how to wash for prayers. The prayers were in Arabic, but Ro could learn them, given time.

The Secret of Kamyonistan

The camel-wash boys finished their morning's work with a Bulgarian garment trailer headed by an Actros. The mistrustful Bulgarian didn't want them near his cab. As they worked, they could hear the panels and rivets of the box body cracking and popping in the heat of the sun. Alongside, dozed an antique bonneted Berliet, one of whose trailer axles was wheel-less and held up by a length of webbing strap. The Bulgarian paid them and they went to the restaurant and ordered kofta with salad.

Eric was challenging Bingo with, 'How can you call the childhood of drugged teenage soldiers, paradise?'

'Although I believe the concept of paradise exists as another country within childhood, it need not follow that a rotten childhood cannot qualify. Paradise will just be less sustained, less frequently present,' Bingo said.

'To be purpley honest wiv yer,' Jumbo said, 'I don't suppose it matters. In a hundred years' time we'll be all dead and gone and no one will know any different.'

'You old cynic!' Eric cried.

'Hello boys!' Bingo said. 'Come and join us. We're off after lunch. Jumbo and I have both loaded at the same place as Norman did. Must have struck gold!'

'What about you, Eric?' Ro enquired.

'Riding shotgun with Jumbo,' he grinned. 'Might even take a turn piloting the old Volvo FH myself. I'm only going as far as Istanbul. Then I'll fly. I haven't time to be traipsing round the Wholly Lorryable Empire with the likes of these renegades!'

'Grenades?' Nuri gasped, startled. They laughed; Bingo looked stern.

'Take my advice, you two, and stay low, if that's possible with two ruddy great camels! I've asked Mehmet here to keep an eye on you. If you get any trouble, go to him. They know you're here and they know you're no threat; but if you set foot outside the zone you'll be challenged by the authorities and may be vulnerable to undesirables, I think. Just use your heads!'

Jumbo downed his *shay* and burped softly. 'I suppose we'd better get going. The light goes quickly now. It's November tomorrow, you know!'

Eric laughed. 'You're forgetting the Afghan camel drivers' proverb: "If luck is with you, why hurry? If luck is against you, why hurry?"'

'Now that's what I call a "working time directive"!' Bingo chortled.

Goodbyes were said and the boys found themselves looking at each other across the table. 'Let's go back to the mosque,' Ro said. 'I want to see it again and the bits we didn't see.'

Mehmet sauntered over and reiterated some of Bingo's advice. Then he asked them why they wanted to go to the mosque. Nuri told him about Ro's interest in the prayer ritual. Mehmet strode off and returned with a thin booklet. Inside, the prayers were transliterated in roman script, that Ro could understand. Beside the transliteration was an English translation. He gave it to Ro and wished him luck.

On the way they met the peanut and wacky baccy vendor and the leather-jacket man who was rumoured to tell fortunes and they exchanged greetings. After parking the camels, they entered the mosque complex and wandered round the outside part. At the back was a courtyard, at the far end of which was a graceful arcade. Passing through the arcade they found a little garden with three palm trees, a clump of oleander and high walls over which bright cerise bougainvillea tumbled. In the centre was a fountain surrounded by stone benches. In wonder, the two boys sat and stared at the beauty around them. Nuri rested his head on Ro's shoulder. Birds sang. Neither spoke. They stayed in the drowsy warmth of the midday sun until the magic waned. Then, silently, they withdrew and collected their camels.

Convoyage

Ro and Nuri established a routine during the weeks of November and early December. There was enough traffic to keep them busy and enough income to keep them fed. Gradually, the sun lost its intensity and the nights grew colder. Nuri bought blankets in the little souk and Ro bought a jalabiya to wear over his clothes like Nuri. The ERF's smashed sump meant that the engine couldn't be run for warmth, so a part of each day's perambulation was spent collecting firewood. In the evenings they cooked outside and lingered in the fire's warmth until bedtime. Their midday meals were habitually taken in the restaurant, where the wonderfully hospitable and friendly Mehmet and his Turkish waiter, Ramazan, always made them feel at home. There were many times, however, when the boys were invited to share drivers' meals. Then they would squat beside the trailers and dip bread into a communal vessel. On these happy occasions Ro and Nuri learnt more of the great truck routes that criss-crossed the Middle East. Inside their tilt, they pinned up a folding map from the ERF, so that they could pore over it afterwards.

Ro began to pick up a mixture of Syrian Arabic from the folk of Kamyonistan and Egyptian Beduin Arabic from Nuri. He even gleaned a little Turkish from the large number of Turkish drivers who passed through.

Towards the end of November, a significant number of stowaways began to turn up in the trailers of lorries. Some were caught during unloading and released; others simply climbed out in search of food. Later clandestines arrived having heard that a camp was developing in Kamyonistan. That camp was hidden in an aborted building project just beyond the diesel and truck-wash compound. It was a half-completed warehouse, which gave roomy shelter. There were no families, just young men and boys with a handful of older fugitives. Some were economic migrants but many were refugees from the chaos of Iraq or from troubled Lebanon, both of which bordered Syria. A few of them were weary Palestinians trying to get into Europe.

One misty evening, Ro and Nuri found a group of youngsters playing football in the diesel compound and they joined in. After that the boys would often spend an hour playing football with the refugees. One of their new acquaintances was a boy of their age called Tariq. He was Palestinian, but had grown up in Morocco. He had been an accordionist in a café band in Tangier until his family had fallen on hard times and they had moved to the rough suburb of Ben M'sik in Casablanca, where he had learned the art of disabling lorries in order to stow away in their cargos. Tariq had decided to escape to Spain but had been flushed out in Tangier docks and had managed to get onto a ferry by hanging underneath the chassis of a trailer, wearing his accordion as a backpack.

Unfortunately for Tariq, the ferry was not bound for Spain, as he had assumed, but for Tripoli in Libya. In Tripoli docks, he experienced a terrifying encounter with the police, but had saved himself by offering to leave with a contingent of youngsters heading for Iraq as volunteer insurgents with the tacit approval of the government. The group travelled on a freighter to Latakia Port in Syria, where Tariq escaped to avoid ending up in a war zone. His trip to Kamyonistan had been in the back of a Turkish trailer that he had mistakenly thought was heading for home. It was outward bound, and he had travelled in the wrong direction.

However, he still had his accordion, and when they crouched round their rubbish fire after football as the sun went down, Tariq would warm his fingers and delight them all with cascades of Arabic notes and harmonies deliciously laced with beautifully inverted diminished sevenths. The sparkling vivacity with which Tariq performed entranced all the boys. Often he played to the accompaniment of home-made percussion provided by Ahmad and a slightly younger boy named Amoun. These three boys were always cheerful and lively. How they sustained themselves, Ro could only guess. Inevitably, there were afternoons that degenerated into a long round of football, camel rides and general horseplay. Then the pair would have to work harder the following day to earn the money to eat.

Some days were written off because of bad weather. If it rained, the cameleers would do running repairs and idle with Mehmet, drinking *shay*. They never ventured into the refugees' warehouse because Nuri was quite adamant about this not being a safe thing to do. Occasionally, on rainy days, they would trudge through the mud to the workshops and watch boys of their own age in overalls engineering truck parts. Ro was fascinated by their oil-soaked complexions and their hollow eyes as they welded and hammered confidently among the grimy paraphernalia of the workshops.

Outside, regular convoys of lorries arrived coated with foul weather traffic film; their tyres uniformly caked with the grey mud of the road.

Ro continued to learn his prayers from Nuri and had already gained some knowledge and insight into the grace and beauty of Islam.

After lunch one very still, autumnal afternoon Ro and Nuri sat once again in the secret garden behind the mosque. The sky was overcast and the light had a pale violet tinge to it. Hand in hand, they watched the tiny birds in the spilling bougainvillea and allowed their world to stop quite still. Even the fountain had stopped. For a moment, not even a lorry could be heard. A sense of mystery enveloped the boys. A grainy, ethereal feeling of wonder drifted through their hearts.

'Do you think we're in it now?' Nuri whispered.

'In what?'

'You know – paradise.'

'It's always paradise when I'm with you, Nuri,' Ro said.

'We'll have to live together for ever and ever, then,' Nuri said.

'Let's.'

'What if they don't let us?'

'They can't stop us.'

'They can.' The boys were silent for a long time. That phrase hung in the air like a winged intruder.

'What if we love each other so much, they daren't separate us?' Ro tried.

'What if camels could fly?' Nuri muttered.

'You wouldn't dare eat your dinner outside,' Ro giggled. Nuri started to laugh. They were soon helpless. There were times when the besotted teenagers only had to look at each other and all hope of sensible conversation would be lost.

Beasts of Burden

Towards the end of the first week in December, the boys entered the restaurant one midday feeling dejected. It was too cold to be throwing handfuls of icy water up the sides of lorries. Besides, the work had slackened off, partly because of the weather and partly because the mechanised truck-wash had been repaired and was open to customers.

Mehmet put two glasses of *shay* on their usual table and sat down with them. He looked solemn. 'I think there is bad news,' he began. Nuri and Ro looked at each other. Would the police stop their camel-wash because they hadn't got work permits? Was Ro going to be banished because his visa was out of date? Were they about to be evicted from Hotel Long-Haul?

'Ramazan was talking to one of the regular Turkish drivers last night. About five weeks ago, a Dutch lorry with an English co-driver ran off the road between Ankara and Bolu. Both drivers were killed. He believes they were Norman and Kees.' No one said anything and there was a long silence. What was there to say? 'I'm sorry,' Mehmet said at last. 'I will help in any way that I can.'

What was there to do? Ro thought. He didn't know how to organise people's deaths. In any case, after five weeks, everything would have been sorted out. Uncle Norman had divorced decades ago and he had no children. He just rented a little flat which doubled as his office. Ro felt a mixture of sadness and indifference. He had liked Norman and he'd been grateful to him for taking him under his wing; but Ro had not grown up with him and knew very little of him until his mother's funeral.

For a few days everything seemed flat. Even their afternoon football lost its edge. Finally, late one night it struck Ro that he no longer had a family. No one in England knew where he was, even. He began to feel sorry for himself and even had a little weep, but he knew he wasn't alone. He had Nuri. From that moment on he treasured Nuri more than ever.

They began to keep an eye out for British lorries, in order to find out more about the accident, but none came. One morning, Ro got up to find Nuri crouched over his camel. 'He's ill,' Nuri said. 'Coughing. He needs antibiotics or something.'

They went to the livestock compound. It was very busy and full of sheep and livestock transporters. 'It's nearly Eid al-Adha and the hajj,' the vet told them. 'I'm just too busy to come now. I'll try to come later, but you'll have to make it worth my while.'

Nuri asked him what the medication might cost. It was going to be a very expensive week. They would have to work hard.

Ro did the rounds on his own while Nuri collected firewood on a home-made set of skids and watched over his camel. As Ro passed the footballers he noticed that a number of new young men had joined them. They were very aggressive and the game looked as if it lacked the usual fun. When he arrived back, Nuri was excited. 'Camel better?' Ro asked.

'No, but I've found a big key in the mud.'

'So?'

'Look.' Nuri led Ro behind the trailer to where he had cleared the debris and rubbish from the door of the minaret. He turned the key in the lock.

'Wow!' Ro exclaimed. The minaret, though merely ornamental, had the usual spiral staircase leading to a circular balcony near the top. It was dark and very steep. They began to climb. At intervals there were slits let into the wall to allow the light in, so that they were not climbing in pitch-blackness.

The view from the top was breathtaking. They could see the rugged terrain of the mountains, with the main road to Damascus winding down. There were distant buildings to the south. The boys could see the refugees playing football in the next compound and the whole of the TIR parking was spread out before them like a tray of toys. Nuri leaned over the balcony rail and stared at the ground. Suddenly, he turned to Ro with his eyes alight and said, 'What if boys could fly?'

'What if?' Ro asked.

'We could swoop over the lorries.'

'We'd be dangerous.'

'We could watch people.'

'Spy?'

'Think what it'd feel like,' Nuri exclaimed, enchanted.

'Look down there,' Ro said, pointing.

'Where?'

'Three lorries together on the left. There's a boy getting out of the cab of that blue one.'

'He's from the camp, isn't he?'

'Yes. What's he called?'

'Can't remember. Yes, I can! He's Amoun.'

'He's got some money, look. Do you think he's thieving?' A hand reached out of the cab and slammed the door shut. 'No, the driver's in there.'

'He can't be that old,' Ro said. 'Younger than us.'

'Amoun's nearly fourteen.' Nuri said.

'I wonder what he's up to…'

They descended, locked the door and hid the key. This happy diversion cheered them up considerably and each day they would climb up and survey their world from aloft. About a week later, they saw Amoun climb into another cab and shortly afterwards, the first one again.

The vet had visited by then and prescribed exorbitantly priced medicine, which they could not afford. They had run out of feed, too, and again the vet was overcharging them for hay. Then Eric appeared. The boys considered this to be a miracle. Eric was on his way to write a photo-article about the container traffic in Aqaba, but thought he'd do a piece on the camel-wash while he was in the Middle East.

Eric was like a breath of fresh air. He paid the vet and helped them to carry feed. Then he bought them winter-strength sleeping bags and gloves. Ro and Nuri dined with him, took him up the minaret and found him 'prehistoric' lorries to photograph. He was, however, unable to provide any information about the accident. Eric fondly kicked a front tyre on the ERF and said, 'If I were running transport, I'd rush out and buy one of these, second-hand, tomorrow!'

'Why?' Ro asked.

'It possesses that superb piece of automotive engineering, the Eaton Twin Splitter twelve-speed gearbox. There's no synchromesh, so you have to match the speed of the lorry to the engine speed using your own skills. It has an inertia brake at the end of the clutch pedal travel, which slows down all the cogs so that you can make really slick upshifts when climbing hills.'

'Most lorries have got synchromesh now, haven't they?'

'Most seem to have automatic now! The trouble is, they don't fit these in modern trucks any more in Europe. The constant-mesh baby has been thrown out with the eco-legislative bathwater. And I, for one, lament its passing; which apparently is exactly what the Euro 3 decibel tester did during the "drive by" test. I cannot think of a finer, more versatile gearbox. All right, I admit I've played the odd tune on them, usually the "Eaton Doting Song" – who hasn't? I've had them in ERFs, MANs, Seddon-Atkinsons and Ivecos. I've done Europe, Africa and Asia with them on long-haul work.'

'But they're harder to use, aren't they?'

'Not once you know what you're doing. Some drivers swear by them; some shun them as "the box of a thousand neutrals". And that's the point; we used to have a choice. Now we have less choice. Yes, I appreciate the need for change, and I wouldn't want to return to starting handles and "armstrong" steering, but it does seem a shame to discard a beautifully engineered and virtually indestructible lorry transmission.'

'Wouldn't you prefer an automatic?' Ro asked.

'No. *Transmission* is the operative word here. I use a Twin Splitter to transmit precise commands directly to the engine and drive wheels. With most electronic transmissions, however, I give the gearbox my commands and it then tells the engine what it thinks I should have instructed, or indeed any fairy story that comes into its pretty little microchip mind. Ever so clever, but I no longer feel in control. Consequently, I stop trusting a machine I've been trusting for years. Of course, it's all a matter of personal preference, which brings us back to choice. Given mountainous terrain and treacherous roads, I know without hesitation which box I would choose.'

'Uncle Norman said these were harder to steal.'

'He had a point, Ro. Now that driver trainers have abandoned teaching the gentle art of double-decrunching, the old Twin

Splitter is becoming a useful anti-theft device. If the absence of synchromesh doesn't get them, the clutch brake undoubtedly will. Fresh-faced crims probably think a Twin Splitter is a surgical implement for separating Siamese twins,' replied Eric.

That evening he left for Damascus. Two days later, Nuri's grandfather arrived in his little truck with yet more hay. Nuri said that his grandfather had only come to make sure that he was looking after himself. The family had become scattered, the grandfather had said, mostly in Saudi Arabia. He only stayed for a day, then he too, was gone.

Ro arrived back from collecting firewood one afternoon to find Nuri slicing onions between his knees and dropping the pieces into a pan of cold water. It wasn't an easy life, Ro thought, as he heaved the wood from the camel's back; but he simply did not miss the media junk culture, the vacuous celebrity culture, the destructive booze culture or the aimless consumer culture. 'We'd better light the fire, Nuri. What does *kibreet* mean?'

'Matches,' Nuri replied. He turned to Ro. 'Shouldn't that be the other way round?'

'What?'

'Shouldn't you have decided to light the fire, then asked me what matches are in Arabic?'

'I was going to,' Ro said, 'Then I remembered that they were *kibreet*, then I wasn't sure, so I asked.'

Nuri laughed. Then he got the giggles and Ro was obliged to roll him round in the dust a bit.

'We haven't got any,' Ro said after a while.

'Haven't we?'

'No.'

'Oh.' Nuri giggled again. 'What haven't we got?'

'*Kibreet*, you donkey!'

Nuri frowned. 'That's not a good thing to say here. It's rude.'

'What's "donkey" in Arabic, then?'

'I'm not telling you. You'll call me it.'

'Why not? You're hung like one!'

'*Hamar.*'

'I thought that was moon.'

'No, that's *qamar*.' Ro rolled him again.

'Look at your hair! It's standing on end. You look as if you've been struck by lightning!'

'I have,' Nuri said, and they collapsed with uncontrollable giggles.

The Minarets of Kamyonistan

Anyone passing that corner of the compound next morning would have heard the pure, clear sound of boys calling to each other in the cold air. One was up the minaret. The other was unloading hay from the trailer.

'Nuri!'

'What?'

'I can see our house from here!'

'What house?'

'Nuri!'

'What?'

'What's "I love you" in Arabic?'

'Ro, come down!'

'What's the matter?' Ro said when Nuri met him at the door below. Nuri leaned into Ro, who put his arms round him. 'I love you, Nuri, more than anything in the world.'

'I love you too, but you can't shout it from the minaret. Not here, it's too dangerous. No one must know. It's our secret. You must be more careful.'

The pink-tinged morning faded into a bitterly cold grey one. By midday, flurries of snow swirled about them. A trio of Jordanian lorries had turned up. Like many imported vehicles, they still carried the sign writing of their previous European owners. These three were ex-Spanish, with yellow, red and orange transparent sun visors bearing printed promises of Pamplona, Palmella and Sevilla. The boys finished early because the truck they were washing was summoned to unload. It was an elderly Scania 142, the gearbox of which delivered a deep, fruity whine, with perhaps a faint hypoidal aftertaste, in low range. It lumbered across the uneven ground spurting ochre-coloured exhaust into the snow flurries.

In the middle of the restaurant was a solid-fuel stove with a pipe that went up through the roof. Round it was a cluster of drivers wearing an assortment of woolly hats, *shamaghs*, overcoats, jackets, jalabiyas and jeans. Most of them were smoking and all clutched *shay*. Nuri and Ro squeezed through to get nearer to the stove. 'They're saying that bad weather's on the way,' Nuri said. 'Roads are blocked in Turkey.' Three Syrian drivers were examining a tiny coin.

'Worth a fortune,' one of them was saying. Nuri translated for Ro.

'Where did you get it?' another asked.

'One of the Iraqi refugees. It's from the Baghdad museum that was plundered by criminals after the American-led invasion. He didn't want much for it. I think he was hungry!'

'What are you going to do with it? Quick! One of the secret police has just walked in. Hide it!'

Inexplicably, the driver handed it to Nuri. 'Hide it!' he whispered urgently.

'He can't be very secret, then!' Ro muttered, and went to get the *shay* and to order some goulash and chips. When he returned he found Nuri standing in the middle of a small circle of angry men. 'What's up, mate?' Ro said.

Nuri began to giggle. The coin's owner thrust out his hand insistently to receive his loot. By now Nuri was giggling helplessly. 'I've swallowed it!' he said.

That started Ro off. The driver was incensed. Mehmet arrived with two plates of goulash and chips. Ro explained the situation and Mehmet exploded with laughter. In the end, Mehmet suggested that the boys stand their victim a meal and maybe recover the coin, to be returned at a later date, *insha'allah*.

Later, they stepped out of the fug of cigarette smoke and melodious arabesque into a green gloom of thickly falling snow. That night they slept in as many clothes as they could.

The next morning Nuri woke up coughing and feeling unwell. By the end of the day he was running a temperature. The following day Ro made him stay in bed but by lunch time the snow had abated, so he ensconced the shivering Nuri in the restaurant for the afternoon. However, Nuri grew sleepy and returned to bed. Ro collected as much firewood as he could.

During the night Nuri's temperature rose and he became fretful. Ro huddled close to keep him warm, but the night grew colder.

In the morning, Ro lit a fire outside in the relentless snow. The windscreen was patterned with frost and their bedding and clothes were damp. Nuri was growing weaker. In desperation, Ro wrapped him up and escorted him outside, propping him in a garden chair by the fire. But the wind was rising and it snatched at the flames. Snow was turning to blizzard and Ro became frightened.

'I can't get warm, Ro,' Nuri groaned.

Ro took him back in, but by now he was wet through. 'I wish the lorry engine worked; we could use the night heater,' he said helplessly. Perhaps Nuri could lie in the restaurant. No, that would be no good. The motel, then? No money. Then Ro remembered Uncle Norman's emergency money. 'It's going to be all right, Nuri. I've just thought of a plan. I may be gone some time.' With that, he vanished into the snow.

He pulled his old anorak round his shoulders, tightened the *shamagh* and put his head down. Hulks of lorries loomed out of the gloom. Some had night heaters running and many had their engines running on fast tick-over so that the falling snow smelt of diesel. Two Turks were burning pallet wood under their diesel tank to try and de-wax the solid contents. Ro could see the lights of the buildings ahead and he made for the freight agents' offices, where he knew there was a currency exchange. Inside the building the air stank of stale cigarette smoke. The windows were steamed up. A few drivers were standing round a stove, their woolly hats drawn down over their ears. Ro fumbled with his English cash and pushed it across the counter. What if the cashier wouldn't change it, or wanted his passport and reported him for having an out of date visa? A receipt was slid towards him, followed by Syrian pounds. He was exultant and nearly kissed the crisp notes.

Ro ran out into the snow. A snow-caked Iveco was being fitted with snow chains by a driver who was wearing a grubby-looking tweed jacket and *shamagh* over his jalabiya. Attached to the front of it by a towing bar was a tilt hauled by an ancient DAF 2800. The driver fitting snow chains appeared to have lost the use of his fingers, with the cold. Ro half-slipped and half-ran to the motel and presented himself at reception. This was where the overlanders had stayed. The man at the desk was reluctant to talk to Ro, but eventually he took Ro's booking.

Running back, he slipped and fell, covering himself in dirty slush. He found Nuri slightly delirious, but with determination he got his mate across the compound and into the motel lobby. The man at the desk looked alarmed and flatly refused them refuge. Ro explained about his pal as best he could, with much miming and pleading.

'You and your friend stay together?'

'I have to look after him,' Ro said, and added, 'He's only got one arm.'

'Guests only,' said the man.

'I can pay!' Ro said, waving the notes in exasperation. The man looked blankly at the two filthy boys. Ro helped Nuri into a seat and said, 'Wait here.'

He ran out and bolted into the restaurant next door. It was almost empty but for a handful of Lithuanians who were brainless with drink. 'Happy Christmas!' One of them slurred, lurching towards Ro. Ro dodged him and pressed himself against the bar, where Mehmet was washing glasses.

'Quick, Mehmet, come! I need you to help me, just for a minute, in the motel.' He explained his plight, and Mehmet eventually persuaded the receptionist to take them. Then they were finally shown a room. Mehmet promised to send two meals over.

Ro undressed Nuri, who was now shivering uncontrollably, dried him thoroughly and put him to bed, using every blanket he could find. Finally, he took his own wet things off and wrapped himself in a blanket. His breathing began to calm as he stroked Nuri's forehead. He felt enormously relieved. The surly desk attendant brought up the restaurant meals on a tray.

'You English?' he asked Ro. Ro nodded. 'Happy Christmas!'

Ro's eyes filled briefly with tears. Had they really spent Christmas Day fighting for survival? Ro fought back a jumble of childhood expectations of Christmas. He then caught sight of

Nuri. His funds had gone on the best Christmas present he'd ever bought.

'Happy Christmas, Nuri!' he shouted and hugged his friend with pure joy.

Long-Haul

By the end of the week, the snow had gone, Nuri was better and the boys were back in the truck breaking ice in the mornings to make tea. At the weekend it warmed up considerably and soon they were washing wagons again.

They noticed an increase in the amount of activity near garment trailers. Garment trailers are tall, solid-sided affairs with low floors and small wheels. Inside, garments are carried hanging on rails and packed tightly. Beneath the hanging garments there is just enough room for stowaways to hide. Even more attractively, the garment trailers loading in Kamyonistan were travelling directly to Paris, Amsterdam and London. At first the most determined and desperate refugees climbed on the roofs during the night and cut holes to let themselves in. Then they grew bolder and smashed the locks off the rear doors. However, most of the trailers had container clamp locks, which were tamper-proof. The older trailers had external back door handles that were welded to a vertical pole on each door, which secured the doors at the roof. The cameleers watched the refugees climbing the trailer doors, using those poles. Newer trailers had recessed handles enclosed by lockable, hinged box-section arms. Stronger trailers had ridged sides like a shipping container and solid roofs. Consequently, the older trailers fell constant prey to the growing number of potential passengers. As more and more refugees made successful getaways, they became braver and attacked trailers in broad daylight while they were on the move. Occasional confrontations with drivers broke out and, once, the police were called, but the refugees had evaporated by the time they arrived.

Then one afternoon, about thirty of them mobbed a Turkish garment trailer as it slowly crossed the uneven compound. One started to unwind the plastic tape put round the locks to slow them down. Two more got up on to the roof. One climbed on to the catwalk behind the cab and cut the red airline. The truck ground to a halt. Ro could hear the driver shouting above the hiss of escaping air. Another dozen clandestines appeared, one carrying a large G-cramp and another carrying spanners. The driver jumped out, locked his cab door and ran to the rear of the trailer where he operated the 'shunt' button so that the trailer could be moved without brakes in an emergency. He then climbed onto the catwalk and produced, from his pocket, a little valve into which he pushed the severed ends of the airlines. Unmolested, he returned to his cab, revved the engine until he had sufficient air pressure and triumphantly drove forward at speed.

His unit shot out from underneath the trailer, which then crashed to its knees in the mud: Tariq had pulled the turntable pin whilst Ahmad was setting the park brake button. In minutes the back doors were open. Drivers emerged to assist the Turk, but by now the refugees, who had long since lost any hope of stowing away on this particular shipment, were just bent on venting their anger and frustration. Smoke poured from the back. There was a movement at the smoking aperture and a small figure emerged from within the cargo. It was Amoun. He leapt to the ground and rolled over and over. Nuri ran to help him, while Ro picked up his little bag with its scattered contents: a knife, a refilled bottle of water, a small torch, a roll of plastic bags and a box of food scraps. Amoun was shaken but not damaged. More than anything, he was angry that his initially successful attempt to stow away whilst the vehicle was being loaded had now ended in failure. Ro joined Nuri in dusting him down. By then the whole thing was ablaze.

The police arrived; then the army. For the next two days, the zone was cleared of all refugees. Some arrests were made. The charred remains of the trailer stood like a shipwreck in the middle of the compound.

As the weather grew milder, work picked up. Some soldiers remained after the trailer fire, mostly boys of Ro's and Nuri's age. They camped in the diesel compound and played football every day. Ro and Nuri joined them and some brief friendships were made. A considerable amount of military transport began to appear in Kamyonistan, mostly in the shape of unmarked shipping containers in military colours, some drawn by civilian tractor units. Also, the boys noticed a significant increase in the number of visiting Iranian trucks. They liked these, partly because they were often headed by ageing American tractor units, but mostly because the drivers were always so friendly and usually spoke good English.

One afternoon they were playing football with boy soldiers when an officer came out and barked a series of orders. The soldiers were galvanised into action and left, marching. As they left, one of them said to Ro, 'We're on red alert – they're going to bomb Damascus. Air raid tonight!'

'Who are?'

'The Israelis or the Americans. Both, probably.'

That night, the soldiers were sent round the zone to enforce a total blackout. Nuri and Ro lay in the bunk of the ERF, speculating wildly about the possible outcomes of an attack on Damascus. Planes screamed low overhead in the dark, but they might have been Syrian. 'If we're killed, we've had a good life, haven't we?' Nuri said.

The morning sun dispersed an early mist. Suffused light reflected creamily from the stonework of their minaret.

'*Sabah il-ishta, ya Ro!*' Nuri exclaimed. 'Morning of cream!'

'*Sabah inuur, ya saddiqi!*' Ro replied. 'Morning of light, my friend!' The alert and blackout continued for several days.

One mild evening, Nuri and Ro arrived back at the wagon to find Mahmout the truck-washer's son, Tariq the accordionist and the younger boy, Amoun, sitting in the garden chairs in front of the ERF, smoking.

'Salem! I don't know how you can smoke that stuff,' Ro said. He was slightly irritated, as he didn't want to be associated with wacky baccy, because it paid to keep your head below the parapet here.

'You should try some,' Tariq said, turning up the collar of his leather jacket. 'It helps you forget who you are.'

'What would I want to do that for?'

'You might want to forget you're not a man.' Tariq toyed with a string of prayer beads.

'I'm not a man; I'm a boy.' Ro's camel staled steamily into the dust.

'Not a proper man, I mean.' Something in Tariq's voice alerted Ro.

'Ha!' Ro replied, non-commitally.

'Two boys sleeping together in that little cab every night. People talk about that, you know.'

Ro swore under his breath, but Nuri quietened him with his hand. Ro laughed casually, if unconvincingly, and tapped the camel's front legs, inducing it to kneel down.

'So what brings you two here?' Nuri asked breezily, switching to Arabic. Ro lifted the water bottles from the saddle. Then he turned to do Nuri's. Mahmout was slashing at the air with a short length of whippy cane.

'To warn you not to act against God,' Tariq retorted icily in Arabic.

'All our work is for God,' Nuri said quickly, in English, to alert Ro to the minefield they were being dragged into.

'Where you come from, men can marry each other, that right?' Tariq challenged.

'I think so,' Ro answered. 'I've never really thought about it.'

'That's against God's will,' Tariq said. 'In Saudi they'd be lashed, and here they would go to prison. They'd be killed in Afghanistan.'

Ro heaved down the saddle and placed it on the ground. He paused with his hands on its wooden pommels. 'Fancy that!' he said. His heart beat fast. He knew the arguments from school, but he'd never had to use them because he kept his head below the parapet there, too.

'We don't really do God laws in Britain, so it's different,' Ro said uneasily. He knew all about the anti-gay stance of the Christian fundamentalists, though; they'd done that in Current Affairs.

'They should be killed,' Tariq said, flatly.

'What? Even if it's natural?' Ro bridled.

'Hush, Ro,' Nuri urged. Nuri was right, Ro reflected. This was a trap.

'These types of men should change themselves,' Tariq said obliquely.

'They don't choose to be like that, they're born like it,' Ro said in exasperation.

Nuri kicked him savagely in the ankle and Ro spun round to see real fear in his friend's face. His love for Nuri overcame his indignation for a moment and he turned to Tariq. 'OK. They should ask for God's forgiveness and settle down with wives and have proper families,' he said extravagantly. For good measure, he added, 'What *are* they thinking of?'

Tariq regarded him suspiciously; Mahmout laconically; and Amoun indifferently. Nuri visibly relaxed. Then Mahmout stood up. He was growing out of his red shorts, Ro observed.

'Just watch out! That's all,' Mahmout said. 'You must be careful. People can disappear here. Vanish for ever.'

'Like this,' Tariq added, unnecessarily, with a click of his fingers. Tariq, starring now in his own mind-film, stood up, too. 'Until next time.'

They swaggered off like movie gangsters. Ro slid up to Nuri when they had gone. Nuri was trembling. Ro put an arm round his shoulders. 'We must be more careful,' he said.

Two minutes later they heard footsteps approaching. Ro moved quickly to the camel. Tariq reappeared, looked hard at Nuri and spat on the ground. Pointing at Nuri, using his prayer beads like a witch doctor's bone, he said in Arabic, 'Do the honourable thing. What future have you as a man, with no wife and one arm? You should go to Palestine and martyr yourself. You owe this to your family and to the cause. In Egypt, you only live a camel ride from the border. You might even get to paradise.' The teenager flashed a glance at Ro to make sure he hadn't understood. Nuri's eyes filled with tears. Satisfied, Tariq left. Nuri shook his head in disbelief.

In the night, Ro held Nuri close. He had become fragile in the past few hours. It took many attempts to extract a translation of Tariq's diatribe from Nuri. He was too ashamed to frame the words, but finally divulged them.

Ro was puzzled because he had been taught about the gentleness and dignity of Islam. He had learned of its compassion, its forbearance and its spirituality. He wondered, too, how the happy, carefree Tariq, with his enchanting accordion playing, could have changed so much in the short time that they had known him. How could he convey to Nuri that he wasn't really worthless, without challenging Nuri's belief in a God who had made him, only to despise what he'd created? Wasn't it enough that he'd been struck by lightning? Ro listened to the boy's soft breathing and knew that he was asleep. In Current Affairs they had pondered the mystery of how well-brought-up, highly qualified youths became suicide bombers. Perhaps this was how it was achieved; by singling out the vulnerable and convincing them that there was no hope for them. The real reason that no one knew why these successful youths self-destructed, Ro thought, would always be invisible, because their true selves were always invisible. Ro felt that he was gazing into a deep abyss and it scared him. How easily could Nuri be tricked into self-destruction by the conviction that there was no future for him, no hope? Ro wondered. How readily would this tender companion of his youth embrace oblivion in the belief that he was of no worth? He fell asleep, resolving to strengthen Nuri's self-esteem with encouraging remarks.

Lost Boys

Nuri and Ro were woken by the din of someone hammering at the cab door with his fists. The sun was up. Ro opened the passenger-side curtain. Tariq was standing there in his leather jacket. A black and white *shamagh* was wrapped round his head and face. He pulled the end of it off his mouth. '*Nuri!*' he ordered.

Ro was seething. He climbed down and left the door open. Torn between street-wisdom and honour, he chose the latter. Squaring his shoulders, he stooped slightly in a four-square stance of defiant confrontation and faced Tariq. 'You can tell *me*,' he said, looking straight into Tariq's eyes.

'I've got something to tell Nuri,' Tariq said.

'You can tell me,' Ro repeated testily. 'If you've got something to say, say it!'

'Not for your ears. Get Nuri!'

'You are a nasty-minded bully!' Ro shouted, stepping menacingly towards Tariq. 'You leave Nuri alone. Keep right away from him. Now get out of here before I lump you one.' He hoped his bluff was convincing.

'We know things that you don't,' Tariq retorted, backing away into the lowered head of one of the camels. He jumped, as the camel half-heartedly bit his arm.

'I should go while you've still got two arms,' Ro growled, and Tariq left. *We know things that you don't...* he mused. Then he grinned, remembering the occasions when they had watched Amoun from the minaret as he crept from foreign truck cabs. 'Time to divide and rule, I think,' he called to Nuri, as he gathered kindling for the fire and filled the kettle. He rehearsed, in his mind, the conversation he would have. 'Do you consider Tariq to be dangerous, Amoun?'

'Yes, Ro, very.'

'Then you'll be alarmed to hear that Nuri and I are thinking of telling him all about the little trade you ply among the drivers. Or are you going to persuade them to leave us alone? Choice is yours, Amoun.' He'd have to modify the English, naturally.

That evening, Nuri's grandfather made a flying visit, bringing a fresh load of meadow hay for the camels, which they stacked in the trailer. The grandfather said he was hoping to return soon to what remained of the family in Egypt. As he left, on his way to the gate, Ro noticed that Tariq, Ahmad and Mahmout stopped him and seemed to be having a heated discussion.

'There must be someone making them like this,' Nuri said later. 'Maybe someone from the camp, or maybe the imam.'

They were washing a Turkish F16 Globetrotter with a fridge trailer the following afternoon when Ahmad, one of the youths from the camp, approached them. He wore an air of self-importance as he greeted them. 'Have you heard about Amoun?' Ahmad asked.

'No. What's happened?' Ro replied, guardedly. 'I wanted to speak to him.'

'He was caught in one of the drivers' cabs,' Ahmad said.

'Who by?'

'Tariq. We took him to Security,' Ahmad beamed.

'We? Who's "we"?'

'Some of the other boys from the camp.'

'I see,' Ro said. 'And I expect Security sent you away with a flea in your ear.'

'No, we have our own Security, don't we. Some of the boys have come back. You know, the reformers like us,' Ahmad said.

'I thought the soldiers had cleared the camp,' Nuri said.

'They have, but we've found an old shipping container.'

'So what's happened to Amoun, then?'

'Tariq made us tie his hands.'

'And?'

'He was caned by Mahmout in front of us, with his trousers down,' Ahmad said, 'as a warning.'

'That's outrageous! They can't do that. Why didn't they just beat him up, anyway?'

'Would that have been better, then?' Ahmad demanded. 'In any case, in Saudi…'

'OK, OK; we get the message. How did you find out about Amoun, anyway?'

'Tariq attends the mosque.'

'Ah yes! The minaret.' Ro said.

'Exactly!' Ahmad replied with a self-satisfied smile. 'What did you want him for, anyway?'

'To tell him to steer clear of the "Taliban"!' Ro said pointedly, adding, 'You lot wouldn't know the meaning of "merciful and compassionate" if it bonked you on the nose!'

'You shouldn't have said that, Ro,' Nuri said when Ahmad had gone.

'Why not? You have to stand up to bullies and expose them. Let's tell the police. They'll have to stop it.'

'No,' Nuri said. 'You can't. The police may harm them, starting with Amoun. In any case, they're outlaws.'

'What shall we do, then?'

'Keep right out of their way. At least they didn't exploit Amoun. He could have been their greatest asset.'

'Perhaps it didn't occur to them.'

Their spirits lifted that evening, when the overlanders reappeared from their adventures. Titania Roberts treated the boys to a meal and chatted with them until late about her travels in Egypt and Sudan.

Business was slack the following day. They decided to try the few trucks in the fuel and truck-wash compound, but Nuri's camel had something in the pad of its foot, so he stopped to remove it. Ro went on ahead and entered the other compound. It was almost empty. He heard a shout and saw a crowd of youths approach, running. Some of them he recognised from the camp. They surrounded him, but didn't seem to know quite what to do or say. Ro looked for Tariq, Ahmad and Mahmout, but couldn't see them. The boys kept looking at each other and it was becoming evident that without Tariq they lacked discipline or focus. Two of them took his arms. One of them said, enigmatically, 'You next, English; you next!'

Then Nuri pushed through the ring. 'Cough, Ro, and keep coughing,' he hissed. Ro simulated a coughing fit. Nuri shouted in both Arabic and English, 'He's dying. He's going to paradise.'

Nuri pointed skywards and told them that Ro had a dangerously contagious cough. He went to his saddlebag and produced a large bottle of camel medicine and took it to Ro, who by now was clutching his chest and rolling his eyes. The youths still had hold of Ro's safari jacket by the shoulders as, coughing, he sank dramatically to his knees. One of the boys let out a snigger.

'It's not a laughing matter,' Ro rasped; but Nuri, whose sense of humour overrode all but the most serious of circumstances, giggled, too. Gently, he prised Ro from the boys' grasp as more laughter broke out, and soon they were all howling with mirth. Nuri led Ro to his camel and they left, unsure of whether the youths were laughing at Ro's performance, his misfortune, at Nuri's transparent attempt to deceive, or all three. What they could be sure of, however, was the way in which this group depended upon Tariq.

That evening, Tariq returned with his henchmen. Ro's heart sank when he saw them. He was irritated by Tariq's swagger and by Mahmout's red shorts.

'You've been to the mosque,' Tariq said. 'Why?'

'If it's any of your business, I've been learning the prayers.'

'He'll make a good Muslim, *insha'allah*,' Nuri put in.

'You can't be a Muslim and sleep with other boys. Neither of you,' Tariq said. 'Even your Bible condemns this.'

'Our Bible says, "God is Love", so it is in no position to condemn love without condemning God. Christianity is already dividing itself over this. Islam might take note.'

Ironically, if either Ro or Nuri had possessed the knowledge and political acumen, they might have argued that the particular sexual act discouraged in revealed texts was not among the exquisite range of tender, mutual explorations enjoyed by them. This was no policy decision on their part, but entirely a matter of preference.

'You still can't be Muslims unless you are prepared to try and change.'

'Are you God, then?' Ro demanded. 'Who are you to decide who can be Muslims and who can't?'

'I've a right to question your morals.'

'Then who are you to question people's harmless behaviour?'

Ro persisted. 'Who are you to misuse the name of God to censor elements of our private lives?'

'These are God's laws,' Tariq snapped.

'So are you his little policeman?'

'Yes.'

'Who's putting you up to this nonsense? The imam? By whose authority are you here?'

'Our leader is from the camp. Soon you will meet him,' Tariq said.

'That won't be necessary. I won't answer to some self-appointed pillock of society. If this is Islam, I'm disappointed. I thought it was about valuing the love between human beings, not criminalising it and destroying it. Islam's beginning to sound, to me, like an empty promise, mate.'

'We do value the love between human beings, but...'

'So what you said to Nuri, suggesting that he should blow himself up was valuing human love, was it? Were you really just coming from that holy, loving place in your heart when you told him that he was a worthless nobody with no hope, who could only better himself by destroying himself?'

'Tie his hands in front of him!' Tariq ordered.

Ahmad and Mahmout grabbed Ro's arms. He had fallen into the trap. 'Run, Nuri! Fetch Mehmet!'

Tariq stopped Nuri and held him. 'We need you,' he said, 'to watch.' Tariq gave a shrill whistle. Ro struggled. Several more boys appeared and restrained him. It had not escaped Ro's notice that the charge against him appeared to have migrated from 'deviant behaviour' to 'speaking freely'. Either way, shame and humiliation seemed imminent.

A space was cleared around Mahmout, who sat on a wooden box, brandishing his cane. Tariq addressed the mob in Arabic. Starring once again in his own mind-film, he led his band in a performance of the video nasty of their news culture. Ro felt his belt being unfastened as he was led to Mahmout. He stood there with his trousers round his ankles, gazing down at the swarthy, powerful legs he remembered pressing against his ears the time he was pinned down in the dust by Mahmout. In a spirited act of spontaneous defiance, he seized the cane in his loosely bound hands and snapped it in two. Nothing daunted, Mahmout pulled the younger boy across his bare knees, tucked up Ro's jalabiya and very expertly used the flat of his hand instead. Ro submitted. Nuri looked on helplessly as the captive's rosy glow blushed crimson. The shocking noise of it echoed loudly among the lorries and seemed to go on interminably. The public nature of Ro's corporal punishment and the heat of the thighs bearing his weight conspired to lend a vaguely erotic quality to his chastisement, so that the occasion became a sort of domestic, adolescent parody of the vastly more serious brutality of the flogging he might have received elsewhere.

The absurdity of this was not lost on Nuri, especially when Ro's enjoyment became apparent. He began to laugh, not with a nervous giggle but with the kind of delightedly amused hooting that displayed total disregard for due reverence. Tariq, who was still holding on to Nuri, tried to silence him but succeeded only in making him worse. Thus Tariq was almost entirely robbed of his thrills for the afternoon. Not so Ro and Mahmout, around whom the excited boys crowded for a closer view, until Nuri could only hear the relentless staccato sound of Mahmout increasing his pace. Then Tariq ordered an end to it and Nuri was suddenly seized with the fear that he would be next. The show was over, though, and the band of youths departed, leaving Nuri to untie his proud friend, whose demeanour seemed to have become rather dreamier than usual. 'If they come back for you, Nuri, I'll take your turn,' he said magnanimously.

The following day, Ro and Nuri met Amoun, whose fate Ro had by now shared. He was able to furnish them with information concerning the possible whereabouts of Tariq's mentor. Amoun confided that he fully intended to stow away on a Europe-bound trailer that evening, and he proclaimed his farewells with confidence. They presented their findings to Mehmet. Shame prevented Ro from speaking about his ordeal to the overlanders or even disclosing details of his punishment to Mehmet; he just said he'd been 'roughed up'.

'They've no right to interfere with you,' Mehmet said firmly. 'You're just boys doing what boys do naturally. They must be stopped at once. You know, Syria is not under sharia law. We take a dim view of religious thuggery here. We have other sorts enough to occupy us. Please don't judge Islam by those primitive regimes that manipulate religion to serve the sadistic whims of psychopaths who want us to believe that they are the legitimate custodians of moral conduct.'

'Why aren't Muslims protecting their religion against such barbarity, then?'

'Trying to stop this evil is like pissing in the wind. Kids of your age in Iran are tortured, imprisoned and hanged for doing less than you've done; that's if their families don't murder them first. But we must find little ways to help, starting with ourselves and the example we set to others.'

'You need someone in charge, to tell them what to do.'

'Ah! A caliph, you mean. And what if the new caliph turns out to be one of the lunatics from petro-Islam, or the Taliban? It's all about interpretation, Ro. Much of Islam is open to interpretation, and it is up to all of us to interpret with intelligence and compassion. Islam's tyrants are those who interpret the scriptures for us and on our behalf. We need to learn to trust ourselves to make relevant interpretations and take responsibility for them instead of trusting self-serving clerics who are so often bent on social engineering and controlling people. Anyway, I'll try to get those boys rounded up and moved on. We'll have to see about the shadowy figure in the background whom you mentioned. He may be dangerous. I'll pass the information on.'

Ro and Nuri felt relieved and began to relax a little after their unnerving experience.

Kamyonistan Lost

Amoun was a determined little boy. Today was his birthday. He was fourteen, but looked younger. For all the wrong reasons, he was entirely in charge of himself. He had learned how to survive and make a comparatively good living. No one controlled him; Amoun was the boss in his life. This gave him more freedom than he had ever had at home, in school or at work in the workshop he had run away from. Selling himself more or less on his own terms made his existence bearable. With an uncanny knack for determining which of his clients were dangerous predators and which were benign customers with ready cash, Amoun competently operated among the lorries, which provided ideal cover in a society where privacy was scarce. He knew exactly what he was prepared to do and what he would not do for love or money, and being clear about his own boundaries, he was able to stick to rules of his own making. This was dangerous work and he was under no illusions about the fragility of his own sense of security.

However, Amoun was not a career rent boy. First and foremost, he was a refugee and an economic migrant. He was not running away from a regime that had imprisoned or tortured him for his beliefs or orientation; rather, he was abandoning a regime that had let him down by falling apart and not providing for him. So he had decided to be a Palestinian somewhere else and had joined some like-minded lads in making an escape. The nature of his work had slowly isolated him, not least because secrecy was essential to both his work and his survival. Today he would celebrate his birthday with another attempt to stow away. The arrival of a rare English lorry that afternoon seemed auspicious. Amoun sidled up to the open door of its cab. '*Merhaba*! Hello mister,' he said.

'Hello mate!'

'What's your name?'

'Bingo. What's yours?'

'Amoun. Are you going to England?'

'Ho-ho! A young stowaway eh? No, I'm off to Doha in Qatar,' Bingo replied, laughing.

'You want a boy, then?'

'Are you eighteen?'

'Yes.'

'Lying toad! You're much too young. Here, get yourself something to eat with this – and bugger off, will you!' Bingo handed Amoun the price of a birthday meal.

Amoun sauntered off and stopped next to a Turkish truck. The driver was removing the yellow Saudi transit plates, from which action Amoun inferred that the Turk was bound for home. The tractor unit was an Iveco Eurotech with a moulded roof spoiler. He hadn't seen one of these for some time. After waiting for the driver to leave, he eyed up the approach route and, checking for witnesses, he knocked on the cab door. There was no answer, so going to the shady side of the cab he mounted the step and peeped in. There was no one in. Amoun ran to fetch his blanket and bag, which he kept ready for such attempts. Then climbing onto the catwalk, he worked his way up the back of the cab using the trailer to brace himself against. Finally, he worked himself into the gap provided by the spoiler. To his relief, the roof hatch was closed and looked as if it hadn't been opened for some time. This would save him from unpleasant driver smells, cooking vapours and cigarette fumes. Next, he climbed down and rummaged behind the restaurant for cardboard boxes, which he broke down and flattened for use at night to screen off the weather. Ensconcing himself in his crow's nest, he then settled down for the long wait.

Amoun did not have to wait as long as he had expected. Before midnight the cab rocked as the driver below climbed out of bed. Not long afterwards the engine was started and the smell of diesel fumes swirled about the unit. Eventually, Amoun heard the hiss of air brakes and felt the truck lurch forward and negotiate the surface of the TIR park. He was rocked aloft in his nest. How far would he get this time? The border? Adana? Istanbul? He would have to find another lorry once he reached Turkey – one bound for Europe, where there was work and health care for everyone and the streets were paved with hi-tech toys, apparently.

At the gate, the Turkish Iveco paused while the police glanced at the transit papers. Then there was a shout and someone mounted the catwalk. Amoun was pulled out by the legs and fell into the jumble of air and electrical susies, banging his knee on the catwalk. The gate man lunged at him with his stick. Amoun rolled out on the opposite side and dodged the policeman. Diving under the trailer, he bolted for the nearest cluster of wagons and wove a route back to his hideout. Tomorrow, he would try again.

The weather had improved considerably during that week, and the following evening Ro sat with Nuri in front of the ERF, peeling vegetables. Ro said, 'I'll have to get some shopping, Nuri. What do we need, mate?'

'Bread, tea, yoghurt,' Nuri suggested.

'And kitchen roll.'

'You look really tired, Ro.'

'I am. It hasn't been easy lately, has it?'

'Do you think of England?'

'No, not really; but it's just hard work being me, sometimes.'

'Think of the little desert flowers, Ro, and bloom where you're planted,' Nuri smiled. Ro shook himself and stood up. 'Right! I'm off,' he said.

He quite enjoyed his little shopping expeditions, though it was always better to take Nuri, who could haggle much better than he could. On the way back, Ro stopped for a *shay* with Mehmet and they exchanged news and small talk. As Ro left the restaurant, he nearly collided with Bingo, who had stopped by on his way out to Doha. It was a happy reunion and Ro's spirits lifted immeasurably at the prospect of a couple of days' café life. Bingo confirmed the regrettable death of Ro's uncle and Kees, but knew no details. 'I hope I'm going to have the pleasure of your company tonight, both of you, at the "Plot-loss Arms"! I'll feed you.'

'Excellent!' Ro said, 'Can you get Titania to come too? She's here, you know.'

Ro passed the familiar DAF as it stood ticking and creaking in its aura of hot diesel and warm rubber. He was whistling as he crossed the parking compound to look for Nuri. It was getting late, and the sun had long gone. A small truck was parked across the bows of the beached Long-Haul wagon. He recognised Nuri's grandfather's truck and increased his pace. Ahmad was there, helping to push the rear door up, the glowing rear light illuminating his face. He reeked of glue. The camels were already on the truck. Ro looked wildly about, catching his breath. 'Nuri!' he called.

The grandfather appeared. '*Selaamu aleikum,*' said Ro and shook his hand.

'*Selaam ya Ro,*' the old man returned, gruffly, but continued to busy himself with the door latches. Nuri appeared, a soft white stain in the failing light.

'Nuri? What's going on?' Nuri stood in front of Ro with an air of helplessness. He opened his mouth and shut it again. His eyes shone. 'Nuri?' Ro repeated.

'I have to go home.' Nuri shrugged. He looked desperate.

'We find him a wife!' boomed the grandfather.

'A wife?' Ro said, incredulously.

'Later. Maybe next year,' Nuri put in with a flat voice.

'*Insha'allah!* You too must get a wife!' said the grandfather.

'Me? Oh yes, of course, of course…' His voice trailed away. What was he saying? This was nonsense. He had to stop this. Bizarrely, Ro thought about how much he'd miss his camel. 'Can't he stay here?' he ventured, frantically.

The old man disappeared. Then a door slammed and the engine started. Ahmad grinned, palmed his ba'sheesh and departed into the twilight. 'I don't believe this,' Ro murmured.

Nuri came to Ro and they shook hands, which felt absurd because they never shook hands, not like this. Would they meet again soon? Ro had a thousand things to say and to ask, but when, briefly, they embraced he was no longer capable of speech. He sensed that he was losing Nuri second by second. Anger and grief surged through him in waves. Nuri turned and walked towards the truck.

'Nuri. *No!*' Ro ran to him, gave him one last little hug, and then Nuri was in the cab and the tail lights were bouncing away across the rough ground. 'Is that it, then?' Ro shouted lamely. He almost howled a defiant 'No!' into the darkness but his fighting spirit had gone. He turned and climbed into the ERF cab, which still smelt of Nuri, and wept brief, bitter tears of anger and defeat; but he held back the terrible, rising tide of grief.

Although he had no appetite, Ro turned up for his meal and sat glumly with Bingo and Titania. Nuri would have loved this, he thought. He felt distinctly unhinged.

'You loved him, didn't you?' Bingo said bluntly. Ro wrinkled his nose and said nothing. 'When I was your age I loved someone. My age. But we couldn't really do anything with it in those days. Just had to swallow it. Ignore it.'

'Did you feel horrible afterwards?'

'I think so.'

'How long?'

'I can't remember. You're resilient when you're young.'

'When did you stop thinking about it?'

'It doesn't go away. A little bit of you is forever missing.'

'How long ago was it?' Ro asked, bleakly.

'Forty-five years, Ro. You forget it for months, years on end, but the dull ache never goes away. Sometimes it feels like anger, sometimes wistfulness, sometimes a dream. Dear God, son, teenage love has a life of its own – and who knows the power of it?'

'Well, that's cheered him up no end!' Titania said, sarcastically.

Ro ignored her and said, 'Like a parallel universe.'

'Do what?'

'It's as if I've stumbled out of my childhood into a parallel universe.'

'It's called adulthood,' Titania prompted gently. 'You've got to be a man some day. Maybe it's time to start soon; look to the future…'

'But I'm trapped in this new parallel universe,' Ro said, his eyes darting.

'No you're not,' Bingo said firmly. 'You're a man now. Look at what you've achieved here in Kamyonistan. You can't stay a kid for ever, matey!'

'But you don't understand. I can't get back!'

'What do you mean?'

'I'm not sure I was ready to change yet. What's all this stupid growing up anyway? *All I want is my bloody childhood back!*' He was shouting.

Bingo took a deep breath and absorbed the desperate intensity of the youth's words, but not their enormity. The anger of their delivery had belied the sorrow of their content. There was something else, though, that unnerved Bingo. Something massive had shifted somewhere inside him. 'Yes,' he muttered. 'If only we could get back. Recover what we've lost.'

In the darkness of that night, Ro's dream of Nuri on the causeway to paradise came to him once again, with its accompanying feelings of separation and abandonment. Then a shutter came down in the mind of Ro, a boy who had just learned that investing in a loving relationship was clearly not a safe thing to do. By morning, the past was already another country.

Shadow Journeys

Ro awoke later than usual. He felt groggy and disorientated. As he set about his routine tasks, the world felt unreal and dreamlike. He felt no emotion. At midday he walked to the restaurant where some of the overlanders were gathered. Titania greeted him and drew him aside. 'We've talked about you among the overlanders,' she said, 'and we'd like to take you back to England with us.' Just like that.

Ro was not moved by this, for his heart had turned to stone; but he was genuinely grateful. 'Thanks,' he said. 'Thanks. I'm going to go home and go back to school and get a job and get married and I'll…'

'Whoa there, Ro! One thing at a time! So you'll come, then.'

'Brilliant!' Bingo interrupted, scrutinising the teenager. 'Here, I've brought you some *shay*.' He sat down, and Titania said, 'We're leaving tomorrow, Ro, so you'll need to pack anything you need. We'll get you a backpack in the souk if they've got one.' It all sounded so mundane, but it suited Ro's state of mind. 'And Ro,' Titania added kindly, 'you'd better get some trousers.'

Ro plucked absent-mindedly at his jalabiya until his fingers came into contact with Nuri's old *shamagh* that he'd worn for such a long, long time. For a moment he felt weary, then he unwound it and slung it round his shoulders. His hair was tousled. 'I could still do my GCSEs, couldn't I?' he asked.

'Well, yes,' Titania said carefully, 'but you'd be a year behind. I'm sure something could be arranged.'

'At your school?'

'I taught girls, Ro, and in any case I'm retired now. There'll be something for you. We have to find you a home first.'

'Home…' Ro repeated the word dully. He looked across the dusty compound to where the hulk of Hotel Long-Haul soaked up the noon heat. That was home, wasn't it? Ro frowned and shivered. He pictured his bedroom at the house that was sold in England. 'Can I stay in the motel tonight?' he asked, suddenly.

Bingo and Titania looked at each other. 'All right. Bring your things and I'll book you a room,' Titania said evenly. Her mind was transported back to an assembly hall on a typical bright morning, where she was seated at the grand piano extemporising calming music to induce quietness in the swirls of girls who drifted and settled in school-blue pools upon the cool, dark floor. She saw their sun-dusted hair and heard the silky choral mist of their singing, 'Shout, while ye journey home; songs be in every mouth…'

She wished with all her heart that Ro could shout while he, rejoicing, journeyed home to the hills of the north. Another old paradise hymn, she thought. 'Home' represented the Kingdom of God, which in turn stood for paradise.

After he'd gone, they ordered *shay* and sat on the veranda. 'I'll have to get in touch with Social Services,' Titania said. 'He's got nothing to return to. No support at all. Do you know anything about Norman's accident?'

Bingo nodded. 'Not much; only that it was Kees and Norman. I've spoken to Ro.' He was feeling very strange. 'He's lost an awful lot here,' Bingo said. 'His friend, Nuri, and possibly, his sexual identity. Mehmet was telling me that the boys have been bullied for their close relationship. I mean, he may yet grieve the perceived loss of his permission to love naturally. And something else, something he seems to have sealed off.'

'What a precious and fragile thing a boy is!' Titania sighed.

'Lapsed boy, I suspect,' Bingo said distantly. 'I wish we could tackle his grief head-on and convince him to be true to himself; to stop denying the pain of his grief. But I don't think he's feeling any pain.'

Mehmet appeared with a sealed cellophane-wrapped magazine. 'This came yesterday. It's addressed to the boys. I think it's that piece about the camel-wash that Eric the journalist did. There should be some good pictures.' He handed Bingo the glossy transport magazine. 'This could be a golden opportunity to open the floodgates!' Bingo smiled wanly.

'Poor Nuri!' Titania said. 'He'd have loved… Quick! Ro's set the lorry on fire! He'll kill himself.'

Smoke billowed across the compound. The pair ran fast, but halfway across it became apparent that the wagon fire was an optical illusion, and that some Syrians were burning rubbish in an old tyre between the restaurant and Ro's truck. The two sixty-year-olds stood there breathlessly before advancing. Behind the smoke they could see Ro calmly pottering about in his little domain, stacking old pallets and tidying the ground area. Bingo waved the magazine in Ro's direction. 'Displacement activities,' he said. 'Let's take him this.'

'I thought he was, you know, ending it all,' Titania sighed.

'No. He'd only do that if he could feel the pain. Maybe that's what he's sealed up inside himself.'

Ro turned the magazine in his hands for a moment, then he walked to the ERF, opened the door and slung it onto the bunk. 'I'll be up in a minute. Just tidying up. I'll bring my things.'

Bingo, who was feeling uneasier by the minute, ambled back with Titania to their veranda table. Ro followed shortly, carrying a little bundle of clothes. He stood on the veranda and squinted out across the TIR parking.

'You'll miss him, won't you, Ro?' Titania ventured, gently.

'I expect so,' Ro said, expressionlessly. 'He was a good friend, but now I have to get on with my life. I need to catch up. I haven't used a laptop for months…'

'Ro,' Titania urged, 'you won't bottle up all your sadness, will you? Your future will be so much richer if you can take all your experience here with you and treasure it.'

'I just want to go home,' Ro responded blandly, 'even if I haven't got a home to go to.'

'We'd better sort a room out for you,' Titania whispered, ushering him away.

It was at that moment that the significance of Ro's predicament hit Bingo in the guts like a thug. He saw in Ro his own fifteen-year-old self. In blinding recognition of his own hidden grief, he sank to his knees, utterly debilitated by uncontrollable sobbing. Ro's situation resonated with his own past history, and this revelation left him drowning in his own grief. Bingo staggered to his wagon and tried to collect his thoughts. He knew now that he was unsealing exactly the same pain that Ro was sealing up. Years of honing his self-awareness on long, dark roads behind the wheel had taught him to stick with the feeling. Bingo identified this as the original pain he should have experienced when he turned his back on his own sexual identity and his own childhood. He wept long and hard for lost innocence, for lost childhood, for lost intimacy... for lost self. The emotional pain was white-hot; more acute than anything he'd ever experienced. Bingo knew he mustn't let the intense pain go, or he'd seal it up again. He struggled to accept it, to make it part of him until it burnt itself out. But it overwhelmed him. Then it wouldn't diminish. He panicked. Bingo's mind began to ponder ways by which he might take his own life, simply to extinguish the pain. It consumed him and wrung him out. Then he began to gain ground.

Titania knocked on his cab door about mid-evening, wondering if he was dining with the overlanders. Bingo let her in and she sat in the passenger seat, gazing out across the lorry-filled compound while he unburdened himself.

'What am I grieving for? My intimacy. My childhood self. The fifties and sixties was not a good time to be a boy who loved boys. Anyway, it was still illegal. And the pressure to be a macho boy was much greater then. Not to conform invited unimaginable shame in those days. So I had girlfriends, too. But really I wanted intimacy with the boys I knew, and fear got in the way. Anything more than brief, exploratory sex was taboo. I felt dirty. Love affairs with boys weren't permitted. Then I ceased my explorations with other boys because the opportunities were no longer there. The older I got, the more dangerous it became. I can even recall the defining moment. I was in the left-hand, back corner of my form room. Around me were the kids I'd grown up with. Suddenly one of them, a boy I secretly desired, detached himself from a huddle of boys gathering at the door for assembly. He approached purposefully and confronted me with, "Are you queer, Bingo?" I asked him what he was talking about. He mentioned a little incident that had occurred between us when we were twelve. "Don't be silly, that was just a phase," I told him. Then the big lie. "Lot's of boys go through it. I'm no queer; I've had girlfriends, so shove off." And then I knew a stunning deadness inside. I know that now. The class lined up for assembly and the shutter came down. I cut off from the pain of not being allowed to love other boys. This was the point at which access to meaningful intimacy ceased to exist. A vital part of me was buried for forty-five years. A silent tragedy.'

Titania sighed. 'And you think that's where Ro is right now?'

'This could be Ro in forty-five years' time if we can't help him sooner.'

'This is the twenty-first century, Bingo. Once he's in the UK, it should be easier for him to find expression for his love. Much safer, too.'

'That's true. I've been out of the closet for some years now and I've seen the changes.'

By the time they reached the restaurant, the overlanders had eaten and Ro had gone to bed to watch television. They ordered food and sat down. 'Perhaps we need to reconvene the Paradise Club and catch Ro as he falls, through debate and discussion,' Titania said. 'You said before that paradise was located in childhood, and that as long as adults reclaim and maintain their child selves, we can take paradise with us into old age.'

'That seems infinitely more real to me now. I believe it.'

'OK, but how do you carry that childhood self into adulthood, when that very transition necessarily involves the destruction of the childhood self? That is surely the significance of this particular rite of passage.'

'I'm not convinced that we necessarily destroy our child selves at all. We may only symbolically destroy them by sealing them up inside our hearts and minds. In childhood, paradise is lost; in adulthood it is regained.'

'Regaining it later is the problem, isn't it?'

'I reckon so. It's one thing to acquire the self-awareness to go quarrying for past experience. It's quite another to tackle that pain head-on when the going gets tough.'

'How can you be so sure that Ro is precisely where you say he is?'

'I can't. I can only look at the evidence and speculate. But the fact that his situation triggered the recollection of my own nearly identical situation is enough to convince me. I think it's possible that this may be, for Ro, the symbolic point at which he departs from childhood.'

'But Bingo, children don't make the transition to adulthood symbolically. They do so gradually. I was a schoolteacher; I watched strands of a child's character mature, then other strands mature as various aspects developed at different rates.'

'OK. Children are not another race or species, but they do exist in a sort of different dimension. However messily the strands of adulthood and childhood penetrate into one another's domains, that interface of the two stages remains the demarcation of different places. Childhood is another place, another country, I believe. I'm not saying that the process isn't gradual, or that Ro becomes an adult overnight. Crossing that threshold is like crossing the equator; there's not necessarily any definition. I'm saying that for some of us there may be definition; there may be a defining moment, or significant event that symbolises the transition for us. I believe that Ro and I share this phenomenon. It could be that the coincidence of denying your sexual identity and losing your childhood identity simultaneously is what causes the sealing up. Maybe it's a survival mechanism: boy perceives real danger in retaining both identities, and dumps them both as a single package, neatly wrapped in the pain of grief for their loss.'

'There is your defining moment, then – the simultaneous abandonment of both childhood and sexual identities. The symbolic departure; the rite of passage,' Titania observed.

They finished their meal and went their separate ways. Titania went to bed wondering if and when Ro would find the courage to look within. She wondered too, how she might initiate his next shadow journey, or at least find him some help. She wondered if Bingo could help him later on.

Bingo was still very raw. He lay in his broad DAF bunk and reviewed his route, his shadow journey. In the past he'd rummaged desperately through his memories, driven by a persistent sense of homesickness; reliving the joys and sorrows of youth in his quest for something terribly precious that he felt he had left behind. After a while he'd begun to realise that it was left behind in childhood. For a long while he'd believed that it was childhood itself that he'd lost, which made him feel hopeless. Then he'd begun to suspect that what he had really left behind was his child self – the self who had known paradise – and that paradise was enshrined in his childhood, as in everyone's. Thus his shadow journey had underpinned the long journeys he'd made in his DAF. At some level, he reflected, Ro's experience had tipped him over the edge.

Kamyonistan

The overlanders breakfasted early. It was a fine day and the mountain sides were aglow with shining drapes of smoking cloud in the glorious morning sunlight. To avoid emotional farewells, they had told no one other than Mehmet about Ro's imminent departure. In any case, the inhabitants were still learning of Nuri's sudden disappearance.

Bingo had awoken already crying. For a moment he couldn't remember why. Then he knew that his grieving wasn't over yet, but that it was nonetheless turning to joy. The world looked infinitely nicer. Furthermore he now had a brand new quest; no longer a quest for something lost, but a quest for the means by which to maintain the precious child self within him into old age. He sat opposite Ro and listened to snatches of apparent lucidity, as he outlined plans for his future. Bingo searched his mind for anything that might detach Ro from the chaos of adolescence, unclip his wings and release him softly into the glory of the morning.

Titania checked Ro's passport for the second time and organised her own luggage. Ro's luggage, which amounted to very little, was thrown into the back of the overlanders' truck. 'I hope Nuri is not suffering the same fate,' Titania said to Bingo.

'He may be better protected if he is,' Bingo replied quietly. 'If he is feeling his pain now, he will be very vulnerable.'

'Let's hope, then, that he has the strength to see it through.'

'The boys must hope, too. They must see that hope doesn't die with youth, but lives on into the night and beyond; that hope is tenacious and brave. Hope is the currency of childhood. Optimism has hope as a denomination of that coinage. After that, we carry it as obsolete currency, of more comfort than use. Regaining the ability to use that currency ensures that we're rich in youthful optimism into old age. Today, I feel rich beyond my wildest dreams.'

'Then spend wisely,' Titania advised.

'When I return home, I'll contact you and help Ro in any way I can,' Bingo replied. He then said goodbye to them and returned to his lorry.

Mehmet drew Titania aside as she prepared to leave. 'You probably don't know anything about this, but Ro complained to us a while back, about some intimidation by a gang of refugees. We've been trying to apprehend the ringleader, a lad named Tariq. According to the gate man just now, a boy of his description was seen climbing into the cab of the truck belonging to Nuri's grandfather as it left the night before last.'

'I'm afraid this doesn't mean very much to me,' Titania answered. 'Do you think Nuri's in danger?'

'I don't know. Ro wouldn't tell me very much about this boy. The gate man remembered him because he and the grandfather were having a dispute about the best route to the Golan Heights, which as you probably know, contains the disputed border with Israel. Apparently, the gate man became embroiled in this discussion.'

'That's very close to here, isn't it?'

'Yes. They'd have been in the area later that evening.'

'Why would they go there?'

'I don't know. I just feel uneasy about it.'

'Well, thanks for telling me. I'll see if Ro can shed any light on this later, when he's settled down a bit.'

Bingo unlocked his cab door. He had encountered himself at a crossroads in Kamyonistan and released the pain that had once diminished him. Now he had to press on, to the Arabian Gulf. After completing his vehicle checks, he put in a new tacho-chart and fired up the engine. There was a tap on the driver's door. Bingo looked down into the brown eyes of a tall, handsome youth in his late teens and he recognised in them at once, that very hope of which they'd earlier spoken. Bingo opened the door. The powerfully built youth was wearing faded red shorts, the impressive contents of which he fleetingly revealed before mounting the step. Induced by such matchless credentials to tarry awhile, Bingo switched off the engine. What was that Afghan proverb again? 'If luck is with you, why hurry…?' He reached for the curtains. An Arab pop song ringtone broke the spell. The big boy reached into his shorts and produced a mobile phone.

'*Alo? Naam. Mash'allah! Shukran. Ma'asalaama.*' He thrust the phone back into the pocket of his red shorts, which he began to slide down over his brown thighs.

'Good news?' Bingo enquired chattily, as he undid himself. 'Yes. We have a new martyr,' replied the boy.

The overlanders were ready to depart. Ro sat near the back. Slowly, the sturdy little truck growled across the uneven surface of the TIR park towards the exit. No one spoke. Ro gazed out at his known world for the last time. He felt nothing; his mind was numb. As they passed under the great arch, its dark shadow fell momentarily across their faces and then the travellers were gone.

In the compound, the dust slowly settled. Arab music wailed from a distant truck cab. Smoke from a rubbish-fire drifted over the lorries and hung in the air. A breeze stirred the canopy of the Long-Haul tilt and it billowed gently and sighed in the drowsy sunshine. On the bunk of the ERF lay a discarded prayer booklet and a transport magazine, still sealed. From the mirror arm fluttered a well-worn, red and white *shamagh* that had once signified the affection of one boy for another.

PART TWO

Routes

The Trans-Arabian Pipeline, known as the TAP line, is shadowed by a road that runs across the Saudi desert from the Arabian Gulf. Bingo drove into the setting sun, heading home from Qatar, several months later. The TAP line road was hard work. Subjected to massive variations in temperature, the shifting desert and the constant pounding of overloaded desert trucks, the blacktop was a patchwork of irregular surfaces, furrows, lumps and ridges. It was as straight as an arrow and, with little to interest the eye, a driver needed to concentrate if he was to remain on the road. A yellow cloud of dust and sand swirled in the road ahead and reduced visibility. For some time Bingo drove through intermittent banks of ochre mist as the sandstorm closed in. He slowed down. The headlights of oncoming trucks appeared at the last moment and he watched for unlit vehicles on his own side of the road. Then the light dimmed to an eerie, dark orange glow. Fine, powdery dust infiltrated the cab by every conceivable means. The temperature rose and Bingo plugged on. Huge drops of rain began to fall, a rarity in the desert. Soon the windscreen was a mass of smeared mud. The sand and dust swirled and snaked across the road in mysterious eddies. Visibility dropped almost to zero. After several minutes the storm abated quite suddenly, and bright sunshine was restored.

Bingo hit the little desert town of Qaisuma mid-evening and parked outside a restaurant in front of the mosque at the eastern end. The front of the DAF was caked in mud from the storm. He ordered a kebab and hoped that the call to prayer would not coincide with his meal. In Saudi Arabia, this meant being asked to leave until after prayers, as no shops or restaurants were permitted to serve during prayer times. This was his first Middle East trip for some months, so he was glad that it was late autumn and not unbearably hot. The restaurant was full of wall mirrors and it had earned the nickname 'The Mirrors', in memory of another favourite watering hole, further back down the road, similarly mirrored within. As he munched, Bingo made a mental note to email Titania and catch up again on Ro. It would probably have to wait until he reached Istanbul. The endless run across the desert lay before him, followed by Jordan and Syria.

Bingo pulled into the parking area at Jabeer, on the Jordanian side of the Syrian border. His customs and transit documents were processed as usual by Mohammed. This normally took little time if he was running empty from Doha, but Mohammed ushered him upstairs into the little office, where his co-extractor of as much revenue as possible was on the telephone.

'Have you got a load yet?' Bingo was asked. Bingo said that he had possibilities in the pipeline. 'Because I can get you a load in Syria. In Damascus,' the man said.

This was a tried, trusted and efficient agent, but getting payments from Syrian freight agents at the other end was not always easy. 'No thank you, they don't really pay enough. By the time I've lugged the load across the Turkish mountains, I'll have burned off the profit in diesel! I might just as well load in Italy and save myself the hassle. It wasn't so bad when you could smuggle diesel through Syria at seven pence a litre, but they've even spoiled that now.'

'But the Turks have dropped their transit tax. That should make a difference. This load pays well. It's clothing out of north Damascus for a Syrian haulier that's too busy to take it itself.'

'What are they called?' Bingo asked.

'Kamyonistan-TIR,' the agent said. Bingo stroked his chin and asked how much it would pay.

Bingo approached Kamyonistan in the dark. Driving rain had rendered traffic conditions dangerously chaotic on the main road out of Damascus. Traffic thickened in the gloom. He changed down a gear, trod softly on the brakes and watched his swaying trailer in the mirrors as the truck lurched from one camber to another. Dropping another gear, Bingo poured in the power. Beyond his windscreen wipers the trailer in front displayed a Moscow address beneath a five o'clock shadow of road-film grime. Its red tail lights glowed dully below. Leaving the main road, he entered the lane to Kamyonistan. A last, throaty gear-change took him into the final turn, and with a screech from the turntable, he swung into the arched entrance of the TIR park. He had not been in Kamyonistan since the departure of the little group he fondly remembered as the Paradise Club. After locking his cab, Bingo made for the restaurant, which he hoped was still run by the hospitable Mehmet. He was not disappointed and ordered *shish tawuk* and a glass of *shay na'na* – mint tea. 'Been any English here, Mehmet?' Bingo asked.

'No. Not for a long time. Kuwaitis, Turks, Iranians, some East Europeans and a few Lebanese and Jordanians. But no Brits.'

Last time, he'd left here to go to Doha, and much water had flowed beneath the bridge since then. On his return to England five weeks later, he had contacted Titania Roberts as promised. She reported that Ro had been found a home and a school and that he appeared to be settling down, if somewhat depressed. Ro had been very unsettled, apparently, by the news that a boy called Tariq had departed with Nuri. It was then that Bingo had put two and two together, and it had seemed very likely that Nuri had, indeed, been 'martyred'. Titania had been very reluctant to tell Ro about this until she could verify the information. She had arranged to take him for a meal once a fortnight and had sug-gested that Bingo might join them. He had managed one occasion, but Ro had seemed subdued and somewhat preoccupied with a piece of homework.

Middle East work dried up completely for a while and Bingo had confined himself to European runs, mostly to Spain and Portugal. One Tuesday lunchtime, whilst waiting to unload, he had wandered into the Spanish town for a bite to eat and spotted an Internet café. A message from Titania ran as follows:

<Hello Bingo. Hope life on the road is treating you well. Just getting over a cough and feeling a bit under the weather. I researched old English-language Middle East newspapers at great length and I finally came up with a snippet that said that a fifteen-year-old boy had indeed blown himself up in the Golan Heights on precisely the afternoon we left Kamyonistan. Then of course I had to break the news to Ro; it would have been wrong of me not

to. He seemed to be resigned to it at first, but then he started to lose it. He came to see me the following weekend and he was in an awful state. It reminded me of you that night in Syria. I hate to say this, but Nuri's death may well have broken the spell and opened the floodgates. Who knows, this single piece of news may have saved him from years of depression or a future breakdown. On the other hand, it may have provided the soil for all sorts of trouble. All this is entirely speculative, I know. I don't wish to sound all doom and gloom; after all, this news will also bring him some sort of 'closure', as they say nowadays. However, things have become more complicated because Ro seems to have gone off the rails. He's been threatened with eviction because he is returning late, drunk. His social worker tells me that the kids he's going out with are into drugs and she thinks he is on the slippery slope. He was doing well at school – he should do, he's a bright boy – but now he's getting hopelessly behind. I feel a bit power-less really. I'd have him stay with me, but he would have to change school yet again. I don't know what to do. I'll keep you posted. Take care, Titania.>

This news had troubled Bingo and preoccupied him for some time. He decided to visit Ro himself. Ro had seemed chaotic and it was very difficult to sustain any kind of conversation with him. Nonetheless, he had shown encouraging indifference when Bingo slipped into the conversation the suggestion that Ro might stay with Titania. Thus began an untidy but necessary transition, for Ro, from his new base to a yet newer one at Titania Roberts' bungalow.

Some weeks after the move, Bingo had visited an Internet café in Rouen, where he read a further missive from TR.

<Hi Bingo. Hope all is well with you. I'm in rude health, thank God. Ro has definitely settled down since his move and his new school is much better than his old one. The really good news is that he has discovered that it is relatively safe there to 'come out', and although he has done so very discreetly, he has none-theless made new friendships. I just hope he does not become too promiscuous. The bad news is that although British teenagers can now enjoy a freedom totally barred to you at his age, there is a drug culture attached to gay culture. This will surely be its

undoing in the long run, then it will be back to square one and have only itself to blame! So now I fear for him once again. AIDS, too, is never far from my fearful mind. Just cross all your fingers. They do say that if you can help a boy to navigate his way from fifteen to twenty-one without killing himself, you're home and dry! Take care, Titania.>

There was no trace of rain in the sky the next morning, though there was evidence enough on the ground. Bingo visited the freight agent's office and then the Kamyonistan TIR office. '*Bokra, insha'allah*, we will load you,' they said. Tomorrow then. Bingo stowed his cab gear and tilted the cab to get at the engine. He had one or two things to look at in the DAF, especially its thermo-coupling, because the engine had been running hot on hills. He heard footsteps. A young man approached; Bingo recognised him as the youth who had broken the news of a 'new martyr' to him several months previously. He strode up to the youngster, clenching his fists beside him. '*You!*' he exclaimed, 'you told me about a boy who had just become a martyr. Do you remember?' The youth nodded. 'Well, let me tell you, I knew that boy. He wasn't just any old boy to be thrown away at the whim of any bloody…'

'You knew him? Wait! I've got something for you. You can have it. It was very precious to him. I kept it to remember him by. But you can have it. You were his friend. Wait here. Five minutes.' The youth, whose name Bingo now remembered was Mahmout, according to Titania, sped off at a run. Bingo was perplexed and his first suspicion was that Mahmout had simply run away, using a clever excuse to facilitate an easy getaway. What, after all, could Nuri have possibly left in Mahmout's hands, or Tariq's hands? Perhaps Nuri's unscrupulous grandfather had handed over the poor little soul's meagre belongs, Bingo guessed angrily. He and Titania had agonised long and hard over the enigma of the grandfather's role in Nuri's demise.

Mahmout returned carrying a heavy, unusually shaped box and set it on the ground at Bingo's feet. He was breathless and his face bore an expression of convincing innocence. Bingo undid the catches on the box. The lid fell open. It was an accordion. 'This can't be his,' Bingo muttered. Then his anger returned. 'How the hell could he play one of these? He only had one arm!'

'No, no he had two arms. Tariq played this very, very beauti-fully! We used to sit round the fire after football and he would play and play. What a martyr that is…'

'Tariq?'

'Yes. How did you know him so well?'

'Just a minute. Remember when you were in my cab that time? Your phone went and you told me there was a new martyr. That was Nuri, wasn't it?'

'No. It was Tariq. He took a lift with Nuri into Damascus. They dropped him off at the road that goes to the Golan Heights. Tariq had contacts there who would pick him up…'

'So Tariq was the fifteen-year-old in the newspaper. Nuri could be alive, then!'

'Yes. I think he went to Sinai in Egypt.' Bingo picked up the accordion. 'Poor little sod. He might have been a rotter, but he didn't deserve this.'

'What?'

'Tariq. You cheered at his death instead of weeping.'

'Of course! He was a martyr.'

'He wasn't, Mahmout,' Bingo said. 'He was a young boy who wanted saving. And nobody saved him.' He turned away. Mahmout put the accordion back in its case. 'You want it?' he asked.

'No thank you. You have it, if he was your friend.' Bingo took Mahmout's broad shoulders in his hands. 'Next time you have a friend like Tariq, you must save him from all this. Don't end up with a bedroom full of bloody accordions!'

Wrongs of Passage

Bingo loaded and headed north, crossing into Turkey at Bab al Hawa and Cilvegozu. After Rayhanli he began to climb the range of mountains that divides the province of Hatay, at the top of which lies the Belem Pass whence came Alexander in 333 BC. This road has some fiercely steep parts with hairpin bends and Bingo patiently ground up the mountain. Coming down in the opposite direction was harder. There were times when, fully loaded, he would simply do as the locals did and engage first or second gear and descend on the exhaust brake leaving the service brakes cool and ready for use. At the top, in a tiny village called Kici, he parked hard against the cliff and crossed to a little café used by Turkish drivers. It hung in the sky on the mountainside and served the cheapest and best kebab in southern Turkey. In summer, one could sit outside with breathtaking views.

Bingo drove on to Iskenderun and Adana, after which he made the long, unremitting climb up the Toros Mountains to Posanti, where a light dusting of snow hinted at an early winter. At Aksaray, he found an Internet café and checked his emails. His momentous news was already nearly three days old. There was a message from Titania.

<Hi Bingo. I wish I could bring you some upbeat news, but things aren't brilliant at this end. Ro has been very depressed lately. Although he's tried to turn over a new leaf and keep off the drink (which he can't afford anyway), he still goes out. Then he returns in tears, saying that he can't connect with anyone romantically because he keeps thinking of Nuri. Poor Ro, he really is still in a relationship with Nuri. He told me that he feels as if half of him has gone. I tell him he has to let go of Nuri if he wants to move on, but I might just as well tell him to swim the Channel. Then to add to his troubles, he and another boy were attacked outside a gay bar on Saturday night. Ro sustained only a

couple of bruises, but the other boy was quite badly injured. Honestly, I don't know what England's coming to. Unfortunately, the incident has destroyed Ro's faith in the so-called tolerant UK, which for obvious reasons, was not very robust in the first place. The doctor who had him X-rayed was most sympathetic, and when I outlined Ro's circumstances, he shrugged and said, 'You know, Ms Roberts, some boys just can't be separated, no matter what. It happens sometimes.' God! I sometimes wish I could just wave a magic wand and bring Nuri back to life. But then what would they do, Bingo? Live in the Middle East? Live here? It's a crazy dream. Anyway, enough of Ro. I'm trying to plan Christmas and I haven't yet decided whether to go away or to stay at home. Which brings me back to Ro again! Take care, Titania.>

Bingo sat for a while. Then he began his message. <Dear Titania, I bring good tidings of great joy. Get your magic wand out and fill a boy's heart with stardust for me will you...>

He left the Internet café feeling light-hearted. Drawing his coat about him against the snow flurries, he made his way back to the Shell truck stop where his wagon was parked. What would Ro want? What would he do with this new intelligence? Bingo sank a glass of tea in the café and then had his hair cut next door. This took nearly an hour because the barber was meticulous and insisted on singeing out the hairs in Bingo's ears with his lighter. Would Ro want to try and look for Nuri? Would wild plans wreck his chances of settling into school and a stable life? He made a decision there and then to make a boy's dreams come true, whatever they were. It was time Ro's luck changed for the better, and if he could facilitate this change without too much meddling and getting in the way, he would.

At Istanbul, Bingo stopped at Londra Camp to have his trailer lights looked at. He crossed the main road by the footbridge to Sirin Evler mosque. The narrow streets were crowded with shoppers and street sellers, but he couldn't locate an Internet café. Returning to Londra, he found the resident taxi driver and went instead to Atakoy. There was an email from Ro.

<Hi Bingo. I couldn't believe your message at first. Even now I don't know whether to laugh or cry. But I'm still frightened for

Nuri. I think he was influenced by Tariq that night. I want to make sure that he doesn't do what Tariq did. I don't want to find out one day that he did it anyway in the end. Anyway, now that I know he's alive, I can't bear to be without him. I've got to try and see him, wherever he is. Titania has been brilliant. I'm trying to persuade her to take me to Egypt at Christmas, but she says that a boy hunt in Sinai is very different from a Nile Cruise or a week in Cairo. She's right. It would be like looking for a needle in a haystack. Hope you are OK and the DAF is going well. See you soon. Ro.>

Bingo took a deep breath and answered Ro's email. <Dear Ro, if Titania has no objections, I will be happy to take you to Sinai on a boy hunt at Xmas. I will make enquiries if you and Titania can book flights for us. Is she coming too? Try and get as long as possible in Egypt. Say two or three weeks. Be good! Yours, Bingo.>

North of Istanbul, Bingo ran into snow, much of which had fallen the previous night and frozen. The old road up the Marmara coast was undulating with steep hills and it was in poor repair. For much of the morning he was held up by a Bulgarian truck, which was stuck at the summit of a hill. When he was finally able to squeeze past it, using the diff-lock rather than snow chains, he found himself at the crest of a steep descent with a glacial surface and a sheer drop to his right. It had stopped snowing and pale sunshine reflected menacingly from the ice. Lorries were jammed nose to tail up the narrow hill in the opposite direction. Disengaging the diff-lock and engaging the lowest gear, he crept slowly forward and inched down the hillside. Weary drivers milled about in the road. If Bingo halted, the trailer began to slide sideways down the camber towards the drop; or, where the camber was adverse, towards vulnerable mirrors and crushable cabs; or slide forwards to jackknife and create a hopeless blockage. It was a horror from start to finish. The lorries on the first bend were cleared by millimetres, then the next descent was steeper and the DAF began to slide.

Instinctively, Bingo ran the nearside wheels into the compacted snow at the side, but he accidentally put a front wheel over the edge. The lorry stopped. It would not move forward, even in a high gear. He re-engaged the diff-lock; still no movement. Men gathered, shouting and waving their arms. Leaning out of the cab, he watched his front wheel to keep it straight. Then suddenly there were dozens of drivers roaring and pushing from behind. A little movement rocked the front wheel free, and the wagon was on the move again with a grateful blast from Bingo's air-horn. Bingo was not elated. He knew that a bad driver gets stuck. A good driver knows how to get out of trouble, but a proper driver doesn't get stuck in the first place. He pitied the fatigued drivers in the road. They probably faced a second night on the hill. Hunched tensely at the wheel, he completed the murderous descent and commenced a new battle with treacherous road surfaces.

Bingo pressed on into Europe, crossing into Greece at Ipsala and pausing at Maria's truck stop for a meal at Feres. Phoning ahead to the Greek port of Patras, Bingo discovered that the earliest ferry to Ancona that he could catch would leave him with the best part of a day in hand. So he decided to visit Delphi. Saving himself the longer, but easier, route via Athens, he headed into the mountains south of Lamia and climbed high to the olive-producing town of Amfissa. Recent snows had largely melted and the day turned warm. Descending from Amfissa, he turned left and negotiated a narrow, winding lane with tortuous hairpin bends before easing the lorry through the tight streets of Delphi.

Parking the wagon at the ancient Greek site, he entered on foot. Being out of season, it was deserted. Not a single tourist coach disturbed the peace. It was a beautiful day and the sun was high in the sky. Bingo climbed to the theatre and found himself in magical surroundings. A misty blue backdrop of mountains and distances was spiked with cypresses and stippled with fruit trees. Titania had been right, he reflected, the ancients had a gift for paradise locations. She had used this site as an example. He would tell her he'd been. His ears ringing with birdsong, he looked down to see his tiny lorry framed by the branches of Mediterranean pines.

In Patras docks, he went in search of another Internet café. He didn't like leaving the wagon unattended here because of the Albanian stowaway problem. Titania's email read as follows:

<Hello Bingo! I'm in a quandary about Ro. He should be back in time for school and he should make time for the considerable amount of homework he will have. He should be thinking realistically about his future relationship with Nuri and should not have unrealistic expectations. He should bear in mind that you may never find him. After all, Beduins are nomadic, aren't they? Just a few thoughts to keep your feet on the ground! Take care, Titania.>

Bingo thought long and hard about this message as he sloshed down his Greek salad with Retsina during the ferry crossing to Italy. He parked up in Ancona docks and found an excellent Chinese restaurant on the dockside and an Internet café.

<Dear Titania, let's just put all your 'shoulds' on hold, shall we? They are simply obstacles to Ro's happiness and fulfilment. Let's brush them aside, if only temporarily and cut through the apparently relevant to meet his immediate needs. He has a dream. Who are we to get in his way? We rescued him from Kamyonistan to set him back on his feet. *His* feet, that is, not ours. Can't we just be there for him – to follow, with him, his natural instinct for what is important to him? Never mind what we think should be important to him. We can create artificial happiness for him, or we can facilitate real joy. This is a boy's dream, Titania. It will be a privilege to take part in it, even if it doesn't work and we come home empty-handed and his homework doesn't get done. Please think about it. Are you joining us, by the way?>

Email from Titania: <Bingo! You're giving *my* instincts a hard time here. However, I will not get in your way. I suggest you two go together. Your task will be difficult; the fewer the better I say. I will watch from afar. See you next week. Take care, Titania.>

Email from Ro, read near Torino: <Hi! I've attached the flight details to this message. We'll be there during Christmas. The plane lands at a place called Sharm el-Sheikh. After that we can go to Nuweiba by bus...> Bingo headed north into the Alps.

Email from Eric: <Hi Bingo! Found you at last. Got your email address from Jumbo. It's hard to pin you chaps down. The mag has asked me for another piece on the Middle East run and I wondered if you could spare a moment to jot down a few ideas, as you're reasonably articulate!>

Email from Bingo: <Dear Eric, nice to hear from you. I'll jot down my thoughts for you if you will be so kind as to dig out a copy of your camel-wash article and send it to Ro at the attached address. Meanwhile, here are my thoughts on the 'run'. There's the Central Asia run, the North Africa run and the Russia run. Then there's the Middle East run. Over the years it is the Middle East run that appears to have captured imaginations, acquiring legendary status and a near-magical reputation. The mere mention of it evokes a sense of adventure, and not without good reason; enough can go seriously awry on a single trip, to land even the most experienced driver in a state of utter chaos.

<Its legendary feel doesn't arise just from individual elements like sandstorms, snowbound mountain passes, epic roadside parties or nightmare breakdowns. Rather, this elusive quality resides in the stuff that binds the whole experience together. It lies too, I think, in the interaction between the driver who has just rebuilt his tilt in stifling heat and an Arab driver who offers to share his meal when the sunset call to prayer has echoed among the dusty palms. The Middle Easter's daily routine is variety – of weather conditions, of cultures and languages, of rules and currencies. Shopping for provisions in rural Romania or Turkey, getting a part engineered in Syria or Iran and sorting Arab transit documents are all part of this routine. So too, are dealings with visitors to the cab door. There are traders, beggars, officials, robbers, prostitutes and any number of folk on the desirability continuum who need to be treated variously with directness, unflappability, respect and wit. His job description ranges from relaxing in the sunshine during customs clearance, to the desperate fitting of snow chains on steep hairpin bends.

<The spirit of the Middle East run is surely distilled in a certain wistfulness to be seen in the eyes of those drivers who were sent down to Dubai or Doha straight after passing their artic tests in their early twenties. Such experiences are amazingly vivid during our formative years, and the atmospheres of Istanbul, Damascus and Baghdad are imprinted indelibly in the young mind. A character-forming start to a long career, perhaps. I once heard a driver remark that he wasn't interested in where drivers had been because it didn't make them better people. He may have

met the wrong ones, for long-haul driving certainly facilitates self-development for those who push through new personal boundaries, who really engage with people of other cultures and who learn to survive on their wits.

<Nothing quite prepares one for the Middle East run. Even a few years on the North Africa run didn't prepare me for Saudi border formalities, desert storms or the sheer magnitude of distances travelled. I have felt changed by them. If nothing else, there is a wonderful sense of achievement to be had at the completion of each trip.

<Many drivers think that the Middle East run belongs only to the seventies and eighties. For the present-day Middle Easter, however, the work is quite demanding enough, without dreaming of how it might have been in the oil boom days. The trick is, of course, to maintain a sense of living firmly in the present whilst remaining aware of other historical dimensions. In this way we avoid existing in some virtual reality, only to miss the real thing. Today's drivers have different kinds of problems to contend with. There are better roads now, mobile phones and plastic money. But rules and regulations have arguably worsened, rates are comparatively lower whilst competition is greater, stowaways refuse to travel shrink-wrapped on pallets, and on-board computer failures have opened up new opportunities for things to go horribly wrong in the middle of nowhere.

<This corner of the transport industry is a vocation in itself. Home by teatime doesn't happen, though home by Christmas might, so long as it doesn't clash with the end of Ramadan. Self-sufficiency is vital, and a cooperative attitude to other drivers is an asset. In order to progress beyond the Bucharest ring road, a sense of humour is required, and it'll certainly be needed again at the Turkish border. There is more to be earned driving a new lorry up and down the M2 every day than there is driving an old one to Abu Dhabi and back, but the choice is one of lifestyle rather than career. Only a prevailingly positive view of tomorrow's adventures will keep the spirit of the Middle East run going. Bingo.>

Sinai

Ro had not flown before, so the flight in itself was something of an adventure. In any case, it was a special trip. For one thing, it had been arranged especially for him. For another, he was on a mission to find someone very special to him. When they landed mid-evening, it was already dark. Bingo's presence was a comfort. He was, after all, a much-travelled man who had been to Egypt before, though not to Sinai. Sharm el-Sheikh was a resort town and felt like one. They booked into the hotel where they had a reservation, made enquiries about buses to Nuweiba and went to bed early.

A beautiful day greeted them. By mid-morning, they were following the dramatic Red Sea coast road up the Gulf of Aqaba in a bus driven by an apparent lunatic. Just after midday the bus pulled into the terminus just outside Nuweiba Port. A line of lorries dozed in the warm sunshine outside the port gates. Familiar smells, sounds and sights of the Middle East assailed them, giving Ro an odd sensation of coming home. Nuweiba was a scattered Beduin town with three quite distinct, separate centres some distance away from each other. A friendly Arab driving a Jeep stopped and offered them a lift for a consideration and took them to one of Nuweiba's many beach camps. Here, they could live simply and cheaply in huts on the beach, with all basic amenities laid on. The sun was pleasantly hot when the pair tucked into a plate of *kabab Halabi* under an awning. Sipping *shay*, the proprietor sat with them and attempted to find out their needs. 'What do you want?' he asked. 'You can go diving. The sea here stays the same temperature all the year round – lovely! Or you can go on a Jeep safari into the mountains. Or I can arrange a camel trek. Also, we have trips to St Catherine's monastery where you can climb Gebel Musa, Mount Sinai…'

'Actually, we're looking for someone; an old friend. You might be able to help us. We think he came from this area,' Bingo said.

'What's his name?'

'Nuri.' Ro spoke up. 'He's my age. That's sixteen. He works with camels and he's only got one arm. His grandfather drives a little livestock truck.'

'I know someone who will know about these people. Come in for dinner tonight and I'll introduce him to you. He runs camel treks here.'

They thanked him and finished their meals. The afternoon was spent pleasantly wandering along the beach. Here and there, camels grazed and ambled about under the palms. Behind them rose the mountains, ahead of them lay the Red Sea, which was smoothly calm and splashed with liquid gold. Beyond, they could see the mountains of Saudi Arabia quite clearly. The warmth of the water tempted them, and before long, as there was nobody about, they enjoyed a swim in their underwear.

That evening, they dined as advised but no one came to talk to them. Just as they were becoming despondent, however, the camp owner appeared with a tall, bearded man in a white jalabiya and impeccable *shamagh*. Introductions were made. *Shay* was ordered. After listening to Ro's descriptions he said, 'I think I know these people. They were a big family here. But I think all of them have gone now. Some went to Cairo, but most of them went to Saudi. I remember hearing about the boy who was struck by lightning, and it was his grandfather I met on several occasions. Last I heard of the boy he was working in Syria, and I'm certain that the grandfather went to Saudi. If I hear anything, I'll let the boss here know!' They thanked him. This was going to be harder than they thought.

The next morning they went into Nuweiba 'city', which was little more than a touristic shopping centre. Here they drew blanks. Shopkeepers and tour operators alike seemed unable to shed any light on their search for Nuri. They tried asking in some of the other beach camps, but with no luck. They returned to their base for lunch. Ro asked one of the youths who cooked if he knew of Nuri. A bigger lad appeared and translated for him. 'Yes. He says that this boy with one arm did come from around here. His family has gone away now. This boy stayed behind with his cousin. His family were angry because he refused to go to Saudi Arabia, so they left him behind. He thinks the one-armed boy went to Dahab. That's the next town back towards Sharm.'

It was starting to feel like a wild goose chase. The following morning they caught a bus to Dahab and spent all day asking everyone they met where Nuri was. Nobody had heard of him. Some suggested that he would probably go to Sharm, where the tourist money was. Ro's spirits fell. Time was ticking away. This was already their third day. Back at the beach camp in Nuweiba that evening, they ate their meal in silence. The temperature dropped considerably at night and Ro huddled into his jumper. The camp owner sat down with them.

'Might he have gone to work with the cameleers on Mount Sinai?' Bingo enquired.

'Unlikely. Different tribe. But he might be working with camels if you say he's good.'

A group of diving adventurers trooped in. The camp owner beckoned to their driver and spoke to him at some length. The driver came over and sat down. Introductions were made. 'I don't want to raise your spirits too high,' he said in an American-English drawl with a heavy Egyptian accent. 'But I think the kid you are looking for is working in the mountains doing camel safaris. I don't know who for, but I think he's out there. He might be doing the St Catherine's to Nuweiba trek, or the 'Ain Khudra and Coloured Canyon circuit. I dunno.'

'How do we find out?' Bingo asked.

'Why don't you go on a safari and see for yourselves? There are Jeep safaris to nearly all the places of interest, but your best bet is to take a camel safari, if you have the time. It's slow and you'll have to sleep out at night, which can be cold at this time of year. Can you ride a camel?'

Ro answered, 'Yes.'

Bingo answered, 'Sort of.'

That night they sat up in their two rickety beds and tried to make sense of their trip. 'We'll never find him at this rate,' said Ro. 'In England we'd just look him up in the phone book.'

'Listen, Ro. It's almost Christmas and we're in danger of setting ourselves up for a ghastly time if we don't do something positive. May I suggest that we do a camel trek and make the most of that experience, knowing that there is some chance – however remote – of us finding Nuri. You'll enjoy riding a camel again and I might even get used to it. Then at least we can go back having done one good thing, even if we have to return and continue our search at a later date.'

'Yeah… Easter, or next Christmas, or the one after,' Ro said miserably.

'Try not to be too despondent, Ro. This was never going to easy, was it?'

They spent one more day asking about the one-armed cameleer, then in the evening, when the tall, bearded man in the white jalabiya appeared they asked him about a safari. 'Yes,' he said. 'You can go the day after tomorrow. Do you need sleeping bags? Yes, and I will bring blankets. You must bring warm clothing and a torch is useful. I will provide food, which Ali will cook for you; enough water – and of course the camels.'

The next day was spent buying bargain layers of warm clothing and making extra enquiries about Nuri just in case. The following day would be Christmas Eve, and their camel trek would commence.

Camel Trek

The air was still cool when Bingo and Ro had finished helping Ali, their Beduin guide, to load the camels. They had been permitted one guide instead of two, purely on the strength of Ro's alleged camel skills. Almost immediately after setting off, they were into the wilderness with just rocks and mountains for scenery. At first they rode with Ali leading Bingo's camel. Then they began to climb and the going got tougher. The wadi they were following was littered with boulders. At one point, cresting a narrow way through a pass, they dismounted to lead their beasts, picking their way down the steep rock-strewn path. Ali stopped to gather branches of acacia, some of which he fed to the camels. They settled the animals and unpacked the loads and saddles. Ali lit a small fire and shoved the tea kettle into the flames. Everything was still and peaceful. For Ro it was too peaceful; after all, he was hoping to encounter caravans of camels in the hope of finding Nuri. 'Never lose hope, Ro,' Bingo had urged, and he repeated this mantra now as Ro voiced his thoughts. The welcome tea was bitter sweet and smoky.

Soon they were loaded and away. At noon the whole process was repeated and Ali cooked a simple but effective meal using fresh vegetables. For an hour or so they walked into the afternoon, riding afterwards until the terrain became difficult again. Once more they led the camels among the treacherous rocks, following a route that twisted down steep, narrow gullies and under overhanging rocks. Suddenly, they would emerge into the sunlight and a new vista would open before them. The shale underfoot was loose and the camels slithered and stumbled, hooting in protest until an easier way was found.

As the light faded, they sought a suitable campsite among the boulders and settled for the night. Ali spread out his *shamagh* to pray, while Ro showed Bingo how to unload the camels and put them out to graze. Mostly, that meant regurgitating and chewing. Soon the camel odours were replaced by the smell of wood smoke, as the harsh, arid wilderness merged into the darkness. Spreading out a blanket to sit on, they prepared the evening meal and ate from a communal dish, using bread to scoop out the food with their right hands.

In the night the temperature fell sharply, and Ro wrapped a shirt he'd bought in Nuweiba tightly round his head. Bingo used a woolly hat. They slept encased in blankets and sleeping bags.

Next day, they doused themselves in very chilly bottled water and Ali made *lebba* bread in the embers of the breakfast fire, using only flour, water and salt. Hot sweet *shay* washed it down and they loaded up to go. The little caravan was apparently alone in the mountains for they did not meet a soul. Ali was vague about their chances of finding anyone at all, let alone Nuri. After breakfast, Bingo handed Ro a soft package and said, 'Happy Christmas, Ro!' Ro had temporarily forgotten. He went to his bag and produced the little 'hand of Fatima' key fob he'd got for Bingo. Then he opened his package. It was a pure white *shamagh* that Bingo had quietly bought in Nuweiba. Ro folded it into a triangle and, using just one hand, he deftly wound it round his head. It was the first time he'd done that since Kamyonistan. He held the trailing end of the *shamagh* between his fingers, and remembered the previous Christmas when he'd fought for Nuri's survival in the snow. It was just too much for him and he cried silently. Bingo withdrew until Ro had regained his composure.

In the afternoon, they had just breasted a high ridge when Ro caught sight of movement far below them in the distance. Squinting into the low, winter sunshine they scanned the valley floor. 'Jeep safari,' was Ali's verdict. The views were stunning, with mountains and hills all about them. These were bare, rocky mountains with little or no discernible vegetation. With the fading light, they began to look out for *hatab*, the Beduin name for firewood, and for a while they busied themselves with straggling branches of thorny acacia. The second night was closing in.

Their third day in the wilds proved to be very arduous as they traversed wide wadis and wound down deep defiles. Ro was tired. Apart from the physical demands of the trek, he had slept badly and been woken frequently by the cold. Then he'd drifted into a fitful sleep with dreams in which he kept seeing Nuri in the distance, but never quite reached him. He ached for Nuri's effervescence and for his passionate kisses. Above all, he ached for his dear presence. For all their increasing disappointment, they were still able to enjoy that sense of 'belonging' to the earth that comes with the wilderness. Their pace of life became natural. They fell into the routine of loading and unloading, cooking and clearing up, wrapping up against the cold and thawing in the sun. There was no sign of camels or people. Ali spoke little English, but he and Ro were able to communicate in basic Arabic. It gradually became apparent to Ro that very few people wanted to be sleeping in the cold mountains in December. Bingo began to wonder if they had been sold the camel trek with false hopes. Boxing Day came to a subdued close. Ro kept his fears for Nuri's safety to himself. He thought of Tariq's observations about Nuri's close proximity to the borders with Gaza and Israel. 'What if boys could fly?' Nuri had once speculated. If only Ro could fly now!

That evening, Ro spread out his white *shamagh* and performed his prayers alongside Ali. 'I didn't know you were a Muslim,' Bingo said, later.

'I was praying for Nuri's safety and asking for help to find him,' Ro said, simply. It was only the second time that he had done this since Kamyonistan. The other occasion was the night he'd given thanks for what he saw as Nuri's deliverance. Recently, Ro had often considered converting fully to Islam, the better to work against injustice and oppression perpetrated in its name. Out here under the bright canopy of stars, he felt, once more, inspired to fulfil this mission. He voiced his thoughts.

Bingo asked, 'Isn't that a bit cavalier, Ro? I mean, becoming a Muslim to influence moral and social change.'

Ro thought of Mehmet's words in Kamyonistan and said, 'Less cavalier than those control freaks who use Islam to justify their sadistic whims by having us believe that it is their job to police our moral behaviour.'

'Aren't you doing the same thing by challenging what you see as their immoral behaviour?' Bingo asked.

'I want to challenge behaviour that is against universal human values, including Islamic ones.'

'Another little policeman like Tariq, then, eh?'

'No. I'm defending what I believe to be right.'

'Tariq was defending what he believed to be right.'

'Don't you think torturing gay kids is wrong, then?'

'Of course I do! Don't forget, I used to be one. I just don't think that making little crusades into Islam to change its tyrants is necessarily the best thing to do.'

'Mehmet said that even Muslims found that trying to change their tyrants was like pissing in the wind.'

Bingo laughed. 'So what did he suggest, then?'

'That we set an example by the way we live our own lives,' Ro said.

'So we change ourselves first, then. You don't need to convert to do that.'

'I do, because then I can issue a fatwa against the torture of gay teenagers, followed later by a fatwa against all homophobic violence. After I thought Nuri was dead, I discovered a lot of information on the Internet. It even happens here in Egypt, where same-sex intimacy is illegal. Discretion is the thing.'

'That's the most sensible thing you've said so far: discretion is, indeed, the thing. A fatwa that attacks something is always going to be an unpredictable firecracker. Listen, throughout the Middle East and North Africa there is still widespread tolerance of this, especially among boys and also among young men who are not yet married, but only if real discretion is used. If you keep your head down – and yes, I know you shouldn't have to, but this is real life – you shouldn't have much trouble. If, however, you decide you want to "marry" your young friend, then go to a country where this is acceptable, instead of lamenting the fact that it's not possible here. Remember that many youngsters here take enormous risks to migrate illegally to avoid persecution.'

The following morning they met a train of camels carrying Swiss tourists. One of the guides thought he had seen Nuri in 'Ain Khudra. Ro's spirits rose, as that was where they hoped to spend the night. There were long silences as they plodded across desolate, sandy tracts among the mountains. They fed the camels with old bread. Ro was relaxing now and had accepted the natural pace of life that went with camel travel. Also, he was so captivated with the trip that he made a mental note to go trekking with Nuri, if ever he found him. Ro delighted, too, in the camels. To him, they were the most beautiful of creatures, graceful and proud. He loved the way they ducked and dipped their long necks as they fed and he admired the visual texture of their coats, which seemed to possess as many shades of brown as the mountains had blues. Ro made a point, each day, of sharing an orange with his camel, just as he had when he lived in Kamyonistan.

They stayed that night in the charming Beduin oasis of 'Ain Khudra, where the camels were watered and where Ro was beset by the tiniest of infant goats that climbed onto his lap and sucked his fingers. They dined on *farashi* bread cooked over the domed bottom of a cooking vessel by their host, a widow who provided them with rice, cheese, olives and fresh salad. That night, with the smell of wood smoke in the air, they wrapped in blankets and Ro swapped words with Ali by starlight. Later, when Ali went to perform his prayers, Bingo said, 'Tell me about Tariq.'

'Nothing to say, really, that you don't know,' Ro replied simply.

'I only know that he played the accordion and had probably fallen into the grips of extremists.'

'I think he might have had some hang-ups,' Ro said dryly, 'along with Mahmout.'

'Ah yes! Mahmout…'

Ro said, 'Do you think Nuri would do what Tariq did?'

'Kill himself?'

'Do martyring,' Ro said.

'I can't see it myself,' Bingo replied. 'He'd survived being struck by lightning, after all. He was a boy with guts and a zest for life.'

Ro smiled thoughtfully. 'I suppose you're right. No one with Nuri's sense of humour could ever be a career martyr.' His doubts nagged him, nonetheless. He threw a handful of *sayala* twigs into the embers. Ali returned and recharged the tea kettle with dried hibiscus to make the refreshing drink called *kerkaday*.

In the morning, Ro awoke to the sounds of little doves in the palms, bleating sheep in the rocks, children calling beyond the bougainvillea and camels grunting. A large party of camel-mounted tourists arrived from Mount Sinai later that morning, and their cameleers took tea with Ali, Ro and Bingo. Among them was an astonishingly good-looking boy of fifteen, who wore a white jalabiya and the two-tone brown and white *shamagh* of Arish and Jebel Musa. Ro exchanged greetings with him but he knew nothing of Nuri, and when the boy pressed his companions, they were unable to supply further intelligence. The boy did, however, show Ro new ways to wear his *shamagh*.

Later that day they met a ragged-looking caravan of camels coming from the opposite direction. At first the eye perceived only the loaded camels and the cameleers' headgear. On closer inspection, however, the European outdoor attire of tourists became apparent, along with strident Italian voices. Greetings were exchanged and once again Ro launched into his well-practised plea, in Arabic, for news of Nuri. His description brought a smile to their faces, but they knew nothing of Nuri's whereabouts.

Climbing through a narrow pass, later that day, they were rewarded with a vista of mountains repeating softly into the distance in several different shades of blue. Bingo said, 'Remember Norman's little talk about paradise, Ro? This is what he meant.'

They stood awhile and watched their camels silhouetted against this backdrop as they descended by the steep zigzag path. Silently, they remembered the two Middle East drivers who had come to grief, like so many, on the dangerous road home.

The following day was hot and they extended their lunchtime to doze in the sun while their blackened tea kettle sizzled in the ashes on the wadi's rock-strewn floor. Fantastically eroded sandstone sculptures shimmered above them. Past and future began to take a back seat in their lives as Ro, and Bingo became absorbed into the routine of firewood, meals, camels and routes.

The final day of the trek started bitterly cold and they were reluctant to leave the breakfast fire to load the camels. By mid-morning, however, the sun had become surprisingly hot and the slow plod to Nuweiba was undertaken in blissful weather. Ro had grown fond of his camel in the few days of the trek, for it was a gentle creature, not unlike his beast of burden in Kamyonistan.

Bingo and Ro sat, that afternoon, on the outdoor terrace of their beach camp. Neither had spoken for some time, when the proprietor appeared and sat down with them. 'Good trip?' he asked.

'Excellent camel trek, but we didn't achieve what we came for,' Bingo replied.

The man smiled. 'Ah! I have news for you. A friend of mine saw the one-armed boy in the port some time ago. He thinks this boy was going to catch a ferry to Aqaba. I should think he was off to join his family in Saudi Arabia.'

Ro slumped visibly in his chair and said nothing. Bingo thanked the man and offered him *shay*, which he politely refused.

'Ro,' Bingo began, 'let's cut our losses and try to salvage something out of this trip. We could go to Cairo for a couple of days. I've been before and I can show you around.'

'But we came to find Nuri!'

'If he's in Saudi, we may have to wait for a different sort of opportunity.'

'Could we go there next, then? Easter or something?'

'It's not as easy as that. You can't just go to Saudi the same way as you can come here. It's a very closed country that doesn't encourage tourism, unless you're a Muslim doing the hajj. The only reason I can get in is because experienced freight agents obtain the necessary letters of invitation and consent for me to be issued with a lorry driver's visa. If I took you with me, they'd turn you away at the border, I'm afraid.'

'Great.'

'Look, we'll think of something eventually. Meanwhile, Ro, what about Cairo? Are you up for it?'

'Yes, all right,' Ro sighed. He was experiencing a familiar sinking feeling that kept on going down, like homesickness.

Shamagh

The Beduin gate man in the beach camp advised that tickets could be obtained at the East Delta bus office, just outside the gates of Nuweiba Port, in the morning. Bingo, however, had travelled by bus in Egypt before and knew the wisdom of buying a long-distance bus ticket in advance. The sun had gone down and the sea was a strange greeny-silver colour. Two camels wandered freely at the water's edge. Palm fronds nodded idly. A diving instructor in a Jeep was persuaded, for a little payment, to run Bingo and Ro into the port area to make their booking.

'Cheer up, Ro! You'll like Cairo. We'll go to the Pyramids and sail down the Nile on a felucca. We'll visit the great mosques and shop in Khan al Khalili. I might even let you ride a camel by yourself! It's the cultural capital of the Middle East.'

'I thought Egypt was in North Africa, not the Middle East,' Ro said.

'It's in both,' Bingo replied. 'Think of a Venn diagram. Egypt appears in the intersection.'

'Who says?'

'I use a simple formula. Is Egypt Middle Eastern by language? Yes, it speaks Arabic. Is it Middle Eastern by culture? Absolutely. Is it Middle Eastern by acclaim? Yes, most maps, atlases and history books say so. Is it Middle Eastern by self-ascription? Yes, it thinks it's in the Middle East. Is it Middle Eastern by birthright? Yes, of course!'

The light was going, fast. Bingo sang out, 'Ho-ho! Just look at this lot, Ro. Bring back memories?'

They had turned into the main road that ran through the little town into the port. It was full of lorries queuing up for the ferries to Aqaba. Most of them were parked up for the night, their drivers sitting beside their trailer lockers cooking evening meals.

'Here you are!' The Jeep pulled into the side. Bingo paid the driver and they joined the scrum for tickets outside the kiosk at the entrance to the bus terminus. Once they had acquired their tickets, they walked out into the road.

'We might as well have a look around and get something to eat,' Bingo suggested. They walked down the long, double lines of lorries. There were wagons from all over the Arabic-speaking world, including Syria, Kuwait, Lebanon, Jordan and Qatar. None was Egyptian, owing to the prohibitive cost to local hauliers. Many of them carried yellow Saudi transit plates front and back. Dozens of goats foraged freely in the road, which was lined with palm trees. Behind the lorries, white mosques stood against a dramatic backdrop of rugged, rocky mountains. One Jordanian, with whom they briefly took *shay*, was doing a regular Amman-Cairo-Benghazi run. A Kuwaiti with whom they chatted was on his way to Dubai with an impressive orange Mercedes NG1933 artic with breather pipe, beacons, stone-guards, Syrian-style camel-bar, top spots, roof-mounted air-con and wide 'steers'. Diesel controls, Bingo noticed, were visible near the port entrance, and lads were on hand to siphon off the residue just as they did at the Syrian-Turkish border at Bab al Hawa.

'This is where Nuri and I dreamed of setting up a camel-wash,' Ro said, glumly.

'No good,' Bingo said. 'You'd be moved on here, for sure. Let's cross over; that café terrace looks as if it might do food and…'

'Hey!' Ro said and broke into a run. Bingo looked ahead and saw a boy wearing a white jalabiya with a red and white *shamagh* tethering a camel to the side of a lorry. He carried a long-handled brush. Ro ran up to the boy, who turned in alarm.

'Sorry!' Ro said. 'I thought you were someone else.' Ro could feel new grief welling inside him, laced with a numbing feeling of desolation. They were wasting their time here. He turned to Bingo and said, bleakly, 'We shouldn't have come. We're chasing rainbows, mate.'

The boy was tugging at Ro. 'What do you want? I will help you.'

'I don't think so. I thought you were someone I knew, a boy called Nuri.'

'Nuri? He's my cousin. Nuri!' He whistled. A boy popped from behind the lorry's cab.

Suddenly, there he was; a soft, white stain in the dusk: Nuri. The world stopped quite, quite still. Ro whispered, 'Nuri.' They looked into each other's faces. Ro had a thousand things to say and to ask, but when they embraced, he was incapable of speech. The two boys held each other as if for ever and ever. Ro was beside himself.

After a very long time he turned to Bingo, his arm round Nuri's waist. Ro said, 'Thanks, Bingo. You've made my dream come true.'

Bingo nodded silently. Nuri then spoke. 'I knew you'd come! I always said you would come, didn't I, Hamid? I never, ever lost hope…'

'*Hope!*' Bingo echoed hoarsely.

'But I might never have come,' Ro said, 'We thought you were dead. Oh Nuri, we thought you were dead!'

Nuri hugged him with his arm and said, 'Why?'

'It's a long story, Nuri,' Bingo broke in. 'We were jumping at shadows, I'm afraid; we'll explain later.'

They secured the camels to a bar on the front of the lorry, thus redefining the term 'camel-bar', and adjourned to the café and took a table on the pavement. Bingo ordered *shay*. Nuri was very excited and wouldn't keep still. 'This is my cousin, Hamid,' he announced. They all shook hands. 'Now that you've come, Ro, he can go to Saudi with the others.'

'What do you mean?' Ro asked.

'You can stay and do the camel-wash with me. You will, Ro, won't you?'

'Whoa there, Nuri!' Bingo said. 'Ro hasn't got work permits or anything. Then there's school to think…'

'It doesn't matter. He can help me and I'll be the one who collects the money. That way, it'll only be me who's officially working, see? He can get a year's visa if he is learning Arabic, I think. We can find him lessons here. It's easy. Ro, we can do the camel-wash again, like in Kamyonistan. I still have the camels. Please don't leave me.'

Nuri's eyes sparkled and danced, and Ro found his

charismatic friend as enchanting as ever. For a microsecond the desperate feeling of abandonment from his dream about Nuri on the road to paradise flitted through his heart. Nuri would feel that feeling if he left and so would he. He faced Nuri and smiled. Nuri took Ro's hands and opened them. 'Your future is in these,' he said, simply.

Egyptian culture did not value personal independence, privacy or nonconformity, and it seemed unlikely that the boys could survive here as a couple. But only through the attempt would they learn to find alternative strategies. They had acquired the necessary autonomy and empowerment in Kamyonistan. Now it remained for them to take full responsibility for their decision. The future lay, indeed, in their hands.

'I couldn't have put it better myself,' Bingo said. Of course boys could fly! At last he had found a way to unclip Ro's wings and to release him gently into the evening in a way that resonated with that fragment of self within. No longer focussing upon its loss but upon the joy of its presence he passed into the pure light to enjoy a brief dusting of that radiance which, like certain music known in childhood, somehow seemed to make the world feel all right again.

Solemnly, Nuri took off his *shamagh* and he wound it round Ro's head with one hand. It slipped over to one side. Nuri giggled and Ro knew that there'd be no stopping him once he started. Then they were both laughing and fumbling helplessly with the red and white head-cloth in the twilight. It was some minutes before the *shamagh* was finally wound into place, where it fluttered in the breeze, signifying one boy's love for another.

END

Printed in Great Britain
by Amazon

79784279R00079